DEVOTED TO A STREET KING

BY

RACQUEL WILLIAMS

ACKNOWLEDGEMENTS

I have to give praises to Allah. Without him, none of this would be possible.

Shout out to my support system that rock with me throughout my literary career.

Shout out to all my readers and supporters. Wow! Book number 14 and y'all still supporting. I appreciate the love.

Shout out to Trinity Dekane, my right hand, left hand and everything. Thank you for rocking with me. A lot of times you put your career on the back burner to support my dreams. Love you Chica.

Shout out to Sharlene Smith. You never cease to amaze me with your constant support. I love you lady.

Adrenna Shipman, lady you are one of my biggest supporters. Thank you, hon, for having my back.

Qiana Drennen, Papaya, Robin, Danielle Ambria and Krystal… Thanks my loves for always supporting and rocking with me. I love y'all.

To everyone that ever bought a Racquel Williams book, I want to say thank you from the bottom of the heart. I love y'all.

PROLOGUE

A bitch could spend her entire life cooking for a nigga, cleaning for him and sucking his old, dirty ass dick and that nigga would still find a reason to go out there and find a bitch who had nothing going on for her damn self. I took a drag of the blunt that I was smoking as I paced the damn living room floor.

Thinking back on my life…. This wasn't the first time that I went through bullshit wit' a nigga. Growing up on the east side, and not having any parents forced me to grow up quickly. Yes, I was one of those fast ass little girls who was attracted to the neighborhood dope boys early on. Their flashy rides and all that money they flashed around grabbed my attention. Before you knew it, I was fucking like a race horse.

The thing was, I didn't know that fucking with a dope boy also came with consequences, like him fucking with different bitches, to controlling my every move. That nigga Jihad was the first dope boy that I was in a relationship with. Things started out good between us, but gradually started getting bad. He thought it was okay to call me all kinds of bitches whenever I would address him about how he was treating me. I felt like there was nothing I could do about the situation, because he would beat my ass if I ever tried to leave him.

I hid everything that I was going through from my auntie, because I feared what dude might do to us. I used to pray for God to take me out of the situation and I guess he heard me, because one day my girl Lexi come running towards me.

"Bianca, they just shot Jihad."

I thought I didn't hear her right, so I looked at her for confirmation. "Bitch c'mon, they just shot him on Candler Road." She grabbed my hand and started pulling me along with her.

When we got on the scene, I realized that she wasn't tripping. Jihad's body was still sprawled out on the ground as people surrounded him. I looked and instantly threw up. He had bullets wounds all over his body. Whoever shot him made sure he was dead.

"I'm so sorry B." Lexi hugged me.

I had no idea what she was sorry for. Honestly, I didn't feel any emotions. That nigga had terrorized my life for the last three years. Shit, someone was looking out for me. I stood there like everyone else, until the police and coroner came to take his body away. It was the day that I earned my freedom back and made a vow not to ever sell my soul for the almighty dollar and some fly clothes again.

A year later I graduated from McNair High School and went on to Aveda Cosmetology School. Doing hair and putting on makeup had always been my passion, so it didn't take me long to learn fast. I graduated with my license and worked at a few shops until I saved up enough to open my own shop with my best friend Lexi. We became two bad bitches with the razors and scissors.

***

I met my husband when I was doing my annual back to school giveaway to the less fortunate kids. He was one of the dudes who came through with book bags, pencils, pens and a few other school supplies.

After the event, he approached me with his cocky self. He told me how great I was doing and during that brief conversation, he asked me for my number. I was a little reluctant at first, because he wasn't my type and I wasn't looking for any new nigga anyways. Months earlier, I got out of a relationship with another dude.

He called me the first night after getting my number. I agreed to go on a date with him at Spondivits. It was no love at first sight. It was more like I was lonely, he was pursuing and after realizing he wasn't going to give up, I gave in and gave him some pussy. That nigga sucked my pussy so damn good, I had multiple orgasms in the back of his car. It was sad to say, but I knew I had to lock that nigga down. I'd never met a nigga who could suck on my pussy for damn near an hour without taking any breaks. That evening, after I got out his car, I limped to mine. My pussy was sore and I had to walk slowly. I didn't want to bring any kind of attention to myself.

It didn't take long for our relationship to blossom into something more serious. I eventually learned that he was a dope boy. Even though I vowed to never date another dope boy, I was curious to find out what he was all about.

***

We started dating exclusively. Then I got pregnant and had two kids by him. After the second baby, he asked me to marry him and since everything was still good between us, I gladly said yes. We had the big old hood wedding, with all the dope boys and bad bitches coming out in numbers. I knew all that shit was for show, because within months after that grand wedding, that nigga's true colors started to surface. I started hearing rumors that my husband had multiple bitches around town. I even heard he had a baby with another bitch. I would ask him about what I was hearing and he would deny everything. Often, he'd tell me that motherfuckers were jealous of us and our relationship. I stopped believing his ass after a while.

Here we are, all these years later with two children and that nigga was still running around cheating on me. True enough, I didn't have any proof, because that nigga was good at hiding his dirt. A woman knew when shit wasn't right though. We used to make love every night and that soon changed to once a week. I'd be lucky if I got any action nowadays. He started staying out extra late and shit and when I called his phone it would go straight to voicemail. See, I was no fool and had no plans of sticking around while that nigga slanged his motherfucking dick everywhere.

It was fucking minutes until five in the morning and my husband still had not found his way home to me, or his motherfucking two children. My name is Bianca and it wasn't the first time my two-timing ass husband pulled those games. Mel, and I had been married for ten years and boy when I tell you, the first three years were wonderful, but the rest was the marriage from hell.

***

I was tired of that shit and, I decided to do something about it. I heard a car pull up, so I quickly wiped my tears, grabbed the bat from behind the couch, and stood behind the door. I waited anxiously as the door opened and he reached to turn on the light. That's when I stepped out and went across his knees.

"Oh fuck! What the fuck?"

I turned the light on, so he could look me in the face. "Damn Bianca, what the fuck you do that for?" He lunged toward me.

"Back the fuck up nigga!" I hit his ass on the arm.

"You fucking crazy bitch! I swear, I'ma beat yo' motherfucking ass!" he yelled as he tried to walk off.

"I don't know where the fuck you going, but I told yo' ass before. I'm not going to be with you if you around here fucking everything. You can pack your shit and get out, for real," I said as I raised the bat again.

"Bitch, I done told yo' crazy ass I'm not cheating on you. I was in the motherfucking trap all night, that's all. But nah, you want to act all crazy and shit. I fucking love you."

"Nigga, shut the fuck up. You fucking something and when I find out, I'm going to demolish yo' ass!" I yelled as I walked off, leaving his ass.

I was too fucking heated. I needed someone to talk to, but it was too late to call my girlfriend Lexi. She was the only one that I could trust with my business. I locked my bedroom door and threw the bat down. I was mentally tired and drained. Fuck, I had to work in the morning and there I was up, acting a fool.

DEVOTED TO A STREET KING
CHAPTER ONE

Bianca

I noticed Mel's ass was on the couch that morning when I was leaving out. I thought of getting a hot pot of boiled water and throwing it on his ass. I swear my ass could not sleep because of all the shit on my mind. I couldn't understand for the life of me why this nigga wanted to cheat. I wasn't bragging, but shit, I knew my pussy was tight and my head game was on point. I even made the nigga fuck me in the ass occasionally and I made my own gotdamn money. I wasn't saying I was the richest bitch in the world, but I was the proud owner of a full up-scale salon and I made good money.

I shook my head in disbelief as I got into my car. I was ready to tackle the day and there was no way I was going to let Mel fuck it up for me. I turned the radio on and K. Michelle's, "My Life" was playing. I turned the radio all the way up, so I could sing along with her. I reminisced back on how my life hadn't always been easy. I lost my mother at the tender age of ten to domestic violence. Ever since that tragedy my life had not been the same. It was then I vowed to myself that I would never fuck with a nigga that was abusive whether it was verbal, or physical.

I pulled into the parking lot of my salon, which was on N. Hairston Road. I noticed that Lexi's BMW was already parked. That was a first, because normally I was the first one to show up for work. I parked, got out and walked in the salon.

"Hey chic, you're here early," I said to her as I put my bags down.

"Girl, yes. I had to drop my nephew Keon off at school, 'cause his ass missed the school bus again. It didn't make sense to go back home, so I came here."

"I know that feeling."

"Girl, you look like you ain't sleep at all last night."

"Damn, I look that bad? It's that nigga Mel again. He didn't come in the house until early this morning. When I tell you I'm sick of that nigga and his shenanigans. I just want him out of my fucking life," I said as I took a seat at my station. I looked in the mirror and saw that my weave was a mess, so I grabbed a brush and started brushing my long Brazilian mane.

She got up from her chair and walked over to my work area. "Girl, are you serious? Oh no. You don't think he is cheating, or anything of that sort?"

"Lexi, come on, what the fuck else could a married man be out doing that time of night?"

"Well, he is a street nigga and you know they do most of their work at night. I guess what I'm trying to say, is, unless you have proof that he's cheating, you might be just tripping."

I thought about what she'd just said before I responded. "Lexi, how long have you known me?

You know I'm not an insecure ass bitch. I know this nigga is stepping out on me. Listen, if a married man, who loves to fuck, suddenly stops fucking his wife, or barely pays attention to her, that means someone else is grabbing that nigga's attention."

"Damn... I guess you're the wife, so you should know. So, what are you going to do? You know you're my bitch and I got your back one hundred percent. If we got to find this hoe and drag her, then so be it. I'm ready." She balled her fists up, pretending like she was in a boxing ring.

"You are a fool, but I am dead ass serious. I am tired of his shit for real. I'm thinking about moving out and taking the kids with me."

"No, not the kids. Bitch, you know how much Mel loves those kids. I can't tell you what to do, but please think this through."

Before I could respond, the door opened and my client walked in. I got up and greeted her. It was my first appointment and it was a full sew in, so I was ready to get started.

"How's your morning?" Jess, my longtime customer asked.

"It's great so far. Just a little tired."

"Child, this is my only day off, so I know the feeling."

I was so lost in my thoughts as I whipped up her hair. I could sit there and pretend like I wasn't hurt, but the truth was, I was in my feelings about that nigga and his behavior. I'd thought numerous times about moving out, but he had always managed to do something that changed my mind. This time though, I was ready to get the fuck on.

CHAPTER TWO

Lexi

Last night was epic. I mean, I had never seen Mel act like that in the bedroom. That nigga's tongue licked every inch of my voluptuous body. I mean, we'd been fucking around with each other for the past year and a half, but last night that nigga dicked me down, properly. That morning, my pussy was still hurting.

See, Mel was Bianca's husband and the father of my god children, but that didn't stop me from carrying on an affair with him. It wasn't my intention at first, but after going through a bad break up with my first love and almost having a mental breakdown, I took Mel up on his offer. For years, he would say little things to me, often times complimenting me on my fat ass. I would brush him off, but one day after the break up, I was feeling down. Bianca was off that day and I was the only one at the shop. He popped up out of the blue, looking for his wife. She wasn't there, so the right opportunity presented itself. I turned the camera off in the shop and before I know it, I was fucking and sucking on another woman's husband. I gushed out in ecstasy as he entered me without a condom. I felt every bit of his manhood deep inside of me. Mel behaved like a savage animal tearing into his newest catch. He made love to my pussy, but most importantly to my soul. I'd never considered being any one's side bitch, until I got a dose of Mel.

At first, I felt guilty, but shit, he started complaining that Bianca wasn't fucking him right. It was a shame, because that dick was worth pleasing. I became his other woman and had no intentions of ever stopping.

***

I knew her ass didn't get any sleep the night before, because of course her man took me out to dinner and then we went back to my place to fuck. I heard his phone going off as usual, but he was too deep in my guts to pay any kind of attention to it.

The ringing of my phone brought me back to reality real fast. I looked at the number, and it was Mel. Fuck, if that nigga kept on calling me here, we were going to get caught. I got up and walked outside.

"Hey bae."

"Hey beautiful, tell me you ain't wearing no panties right now." He chuckled with his nasty self.

"You better quit playing. You know I get wet real fast," I joked back.

"That's what I want. Shit, I want to stick my tongue up in that tight ass pussy right now."

"Mel, stop please," I said as I patted my pussy. That nigga was really tripping. He knew I was weak for that dick and would not think twice about leaving work.

"You like that, don't you? I'll be over tonight for another round of last night."

"Listen, we goin' have to do something different. Bianca's talking about moving out and taking your kids with her."

"That bitch ain't goin' do shit. She been using that shit for years, trying to manipulate me," he replied with his cocky ass.

That was one of the things that I liked about him. He didn't give a fuck about what came out of his mouth.

"A'ight boo. I'm just putting you on game, so you can be a few steps ahead of her. You know you my boo."

"You know I appreciate you. How is you and my baby feeling?"

"Huh?" He caught me off guard.

"You and my little one that's growing in your stomach."

"Forgive me babe, it's still early. We are both doing great. The vomiting kind of slowed down these days. Anything else, I can deal with." I rubbed my stomach and smiled at the thought of Mel's seed growing inside of me.

See, it had been a struggle trying to have a baby. Twice I came close, but ended up having miscarriages. That time around, I was being extra careful. To be honest, it wasn't my intention to get pregnant by my best friend's husband, but shit happened and there I was pregnant. At first, I hid my pregnancy from Bianca he, only because I was trying to figure out my story about who I was pregnant by. Eventually I told her, but of course she didn't know who the daddy was. She was even talking about giving me a baby shower at the shop.

"Well, that's good to hear. Listen I got to run, but I will hit you back on yo' lunch break."

"A'ight babes."

I hung the phone up, got out of the car and walked back into the salon. Bianca was still tending to her client, which was a good thing. I didn't feel like entertaining her. Lately, I'd been thinking about getting my own shop. I didn't want to raise any kind of suspicion, because she and I had been in business for years and everything was going good business wise.

"Girl, who was that on the phone? I see how you hurried out of here." She surprised me.

"Child, that was nothing and nobody important."

"Hmm... Really? I think you're holding out on me. I see how you walk around here smiling from ear to ear, especially when that phone rings. So, who is he bitch? Is he the daddy? When will I meet him?"

"Girl, like I said, it's a nobody. I mean, I got that friend that I give the pussy to from time to time, but we ain't on nothing serious. Shit, just happened"

"Why? Is he married? I told yo' ass about messing with people's husbands. I hope you ain't pregnant by some woman's man. Karma's gonna get yo' ass once you find yo' own husband."

"I ain't messing wit' nobody's husband, but if I do, trust me that wouldn't be my problem. Shit to be real, if that bitch was fucking and sucking her husband right, he wouldn't be trying to get into these drawers."

"Really, that's how you see it? I mean, I know I please my husband to the fullest, but that doesn't stop him from going around screwing. You just saying that 'cause you ain't never been married."

"Girl, I am so sorry. You know I didn't mean it like that. Mel is just a dog. I'll be happy when you divorce his ass and find you a good man." I tried to clean it up really quick.

"I'm good. You my best friend and I just want you to be happy and stop selling yourself short. There are good men out here who are waiting to wife a woman like you. Just don't miss your blessings by messing around with these old duck ass niggas." She walked off to go tend to her client.

Damn bitch, if you know so damn much, why is your husband sleeping around with me every chance he gets? I thought as I watched her walk off.

CHAPTER THREE

Bianca

It was Sunday and I was happy to be off and far away from that damn salon. Yesterday was a rough day. From the time that I walked in the salon at eight am, until eleven pm, I'd been on my feet. The shop was jumping and we made a killing, but I was tired as hell by the time I hopped my ass out. I could tell that Lexi was beat also. Shit, I couldn't complain, because it was money.

I heard Mel moving around downstairs. I'd been trying my best to avoid him the best way I could after the other night. I told his ass that I was done and I wanted him out, but for some crazy reason, that nigga didn't get the drift. I grabbed the pile of laundry I had on the floor and walked down the stairs. Sunday was my laundry day, since that was the only day that I had free.

Bap! Bap! I felt blows to my face. I fell backwards on the steps and the clothes flew out of my hands. I hit my head hard, so my first response was to check to see if I was bleeding.

"Bitch, what the fuck you said, you goin' do wit' my kids?" My husband was kneeling on top of me with his huge manly hands wrapped around my neck.

"Get off me!" I screamed, trying to force his hands away. I quickly realized that I wasn't strong enough to accomplish that task.

He started pounding my face. "No, stop! Stop. You're going to kill, me!" I screamed out.

"That wouldn't be a bad idea after all, huh? Bitch, you ain't goin' nowhere and my kids damn sure ain't leaving." He got up off me and spit dead in my face. I balled up in the fetal position and cried.

I heard him walk off, cussing and calling me all kind of bitches. At that moment, I managed to get myself up and ran up the stairs. I locked myself in my room and buried my head in my pillow. My face was hurting like hell, but it was my heart that was broken in a million pieces.

I tried racking my brain about what that nigga was talking about. I'd been doing a great job of avoiding him, so why the fuck would he say that? I couldn't come up with an explanation and truthfully, my head was hurting too damn much. The more I laid there, the angrier I became. I jumped out of the bed and ran to the mirror. The sight in front of me was fucking unbelievable. I could barely open my eyes, and the little I could see, was just horrible. My face was swollen and my dark skin was a bright purple tone. Tears rolled down my cheeks and stung the open cuts on my face.

I walked back into my room and dialed 911. I was too ashamed to get anyone involved, but there was no way I was going to let him get away with what he'd done.

***

"Ma'am, do you know who did this to you?"

"Yes," I told the detective. "My husband did this to me."

"What is your husband's name and is he still in the home?"

"His name is Melvin Brown and I'm not sure if he is here. If his car is not outside, then he's not at home."

After searching the house, it was realized that he was gone. That old, coward ass nigga did not have the balls to stick around after what he had done.

"The ambulance is here to take you to the hospital ma'am."

"Thanks," I said after I locked the door to the house. I was relieved that had happened when the kids were on summer break with my mom's aunt in

Miami. The last thing I needed was them seeing their mama getting her ass beat.

***

After getting examined by the doctor, and getting x-rayed, I sat in the room waiting to get the results. My phone started ringing and I realized it was Lexi. "Hey boo."

"Girl, I been trying to call you. I wanted to see if you wanted to go grab a bite."

I didn't respond. I just bust out crying.

"Bianca, what's wrong? Are you ok?" she asked, sounding concerned.

"No, I'm at the hospital."

"Hospital? What, you feeling ill or something?"

"No, Mel beat me up pretty bad tonight."

"Say what? You can't be serious. So, who is there with you?"

I was irritated, with her and all these damn questions. "I'm here by myself. I'm waiting on the results of the x-ray, to see if I have any broke bones."

"Child no. I'm on my way up there now."

I hung the phone up and eased my head back on the bed. The pain was easing up because of that 800 mg of Motrin, they gave me. I was more concerned with the mental pain that I was feeling.

CHAPTER FOUR

LEXI

Soon as I hung the phone up, I turned to Mel. He was sitting on the edge of my bed. "She's at the hospital."

"Tell me what she said to you."

I was feeling it for my boo. I knew he wasn't a woman beater and she must've pushed him too far. I knew how ignorant Bianca could get at times.

"She just said you beat her up and she was waiting on the doctor to give her the results of the x-ray. She thinks she might have broken bones."

He jumped up off the bed and rubbed his hand over his face. "That bitch is lying bae. All I did was push the bitch off me, because she attacked me first, accusing me of cheating and shit."

I got up and walked over to him. I wrapped my arms around my man and tried to console him. Obviously, he was stressed out behind everything.

"Did she say anything about calling the police? You know that bitch love the police."

"No, she didn't mention anything about the police. I'ma get dressed and run up there to see her. Hopefully I can talk some sense into her."

"Thank you, baby. Come here." He pulled me closer to him, held me and kissed me on the forehead.

"You do know I love you, right? This a little bump in the road and I promise after this shit, I'm getting a divorce and we can finally raise our baby together." He rubbed my stomach.

I took a long breath. It wasn't that I didn't believe what he was saying. It was that I knew it was not as easy as he was saying. I knew Bianca and I knew she was going to get him for every fucking dime.

"A'ight babe. Just lay low until I call you to let you know if everything's good." I kissed Mel as I pulled off in the brand-new BMW he'd bought me as an early birthday gift. On the way to the hospital, I tried to come up with what I was going to say to Bianca. We'd been friends long enough for me to know that she was no dummy and would catch on to things fast. I rubbed my stomach. I swear, I would be happy when my baby made its entrance in the world. Mommy and daddy were going to be so damn happy. I smiled at the thought of seeing Mel with his baby.

The honking of a car horn pulled me back into reality. I quickly swerved my car back into my lane. I pulled into the hospital parking lot and quickly parked. I got the room number and got on the elevator. I tried to prepare myself mentally for the show that I was about to put on. I knocked on the door before I entered.

"Come in," I heard Bianca barely whisper.

I walked in and noticed her face right away. It was bandaged up, but I still could see that it was swollen and bruised up. She looked like someone had been stomping on her. "Hey boo."

It took me a second to regain my composure.

"Hey love. How you feeling?" I tried to swallow. It seemed like something was stuck in my throat.

"I'm here. The doctor said my jaw bone is broken," she said through clenched teeth.

I sat at the edge of the bed. I couldn't stop staring at her face. There was no way Mel had done that to her. Maybe she hurt herself after she realized that he didn't want her anymore. "Damn, I know you said Mel did this, but are you sure this wasn't an intruder?" I rubbed her leg so she would know that I was right there with her.

"Lexi, I know I'm beat up pretty bad, but that has nothing to do with my mental state. Yes, it was Melvin; the man that I've been married to for years. I begged him for mercy while he pounded my head into the wood floor. Matter of fact, the police are looking for his ass right now."

I jumped at the mention of the police, but quickly caught myself. I took a few seconds to get myself together. "The police?" I asked in a soft tone.

"Yes, the police. You think I was goin' let that nigga put his hands on me and I don't press charges on him? That is why I need to get a gun, 'cause if I had one, it would've been the coroner picking up his ass off the floor."

I was feeling very uneasy, sitting there listening to her talking about getting my baby daddy locked up.

"Bianca, do you think that's something you want to do? I mean e'erybody and their mama goin' be up in yo' business. You can imagine what the conversation goin' be at the shop?"

"Lexi, to be honest, I don't give a fuck about what a bitch, or nigga say about me. I'm the one with a busted face and broken jaw bone, not them. Matter a fact, who fucking side are you on? You sound like you are team Melvin right about now."

"Bianca, stop talking foolishness. I am your friend, but over the years, I've gotten to know Mel and I know that he loves you dearly. Ain't no way he could've done this to you."

"Well, obviously, you don't know him at all, because he did this shit to me. I have no reason to lie to you. Like I said, I can't wait for the damn police to pick his ass up."

"I'm sorry Bianca. I never intended to make you angry. To be honest, I'm just trying to make some kind of sense of all this shit."

I felt my phone vibrating. I picked it up and realized that it was Mel. I pressed ignore. I planned to call him as soon as I left.

"So, how long are they gonna keep you in here?"

"I'm not sure. I just pray to God the police find his ass soon. I am going to get a restraining order against him as soon as I get out of here."

"Alright, well take care of yourself. I will be at the shop tomorrow, holding things down. Call me if you need me chick."

I reached over and gave her a hug. "A'ight babe."

I hurriedly walked out of the room and got on the elevator. I dialed Mel's number.

"Hey babe, I was starting to think something was wrong with you."

"No, I was busy trying to convince your wife that it wasn't you that busted her face up like that."

"Say what? Bae, I told you exactly what happened. That bitch lying if she says different."

My head was pounding. I got off the elevator and walked to my car. There I was caught up in the middle of some shit that had nothing to do with me. All I wanted was the fucking man, not all his fucking drama.

"Well, the police are looking for you. I say turn yourself in, bond out, then get a divorce. I damn sure ain't goin' stress me and my unborn child out over that bitch and her antics.

"I'm at the house waiting on you."

"Alright, I'm on the way."

***

"That bitch face is swollen and she said her jaw bone is broken."

"I swear babe, that bitch's just trying to set me up. I bet you it's because I told her I was done with her ass. I swear, I fucking hate that bitch."

"You need to calm down and think rationally. She wants you to be upset and do something stupid." I walked over to him and started massaging his back.

He pulled me in front of him. "You know babe, fuck her. Right now, it's about me and you. I want you to know how much I love you and I'm looking forward to spending the rest of my life with you."

I kissed him on the lips. "Fuck the small talk nigga and give me that dick." I was horny as hell and Mel was teasing a bitch. I wasn't the type to chase the dick, but that nigga was turning me on with all that love talk. I waited for months to hear him say those magic words and finally, he did.

"Be careful what you ask for. You just might just get it," Mel shot back with laughter.

Hell, I wasn't in the fucking laughing mood. If my hormones could talk they'd say, nigga quit playing and fuck the shit out of me. "Fuck that shit nigga, with your scared ass," I called his bluff.

"I got your scared ass." Next thing I knew, Mel was unzipping his pants. My eyes saw the glory. His shit was hanging like a tree trunk. I couldn't help myself. I had to grab it to make sure it was real.

"That's what I'm talking about." I jacked Mel's dick until it was hard, because I didn't want no limp dick up in my pussy.

"Nah bitch, this is what I'm talking about." Mel grabbed me by the neck and threw me up against the bed. My back was arched, while his right hand moved up my skirt, between my legs. "This is what you want?" His finger slipped into my wetness. I couldn't front. Mel's aggressiveness turned me the fuck on.

"I don't give a fuck what you call me, just fuck me." At the time, I wasn't too proud to beg.

"Hurry up." I spread my legs. Fuck a finger. I wanted the dick. I didn't care if it was a quickie. My insides knew what I wanted and I knew what I needed.

"I'ma give it to you bitch." Mel jammed his dick into my pussy.

"Fuck this pussy!" I wanted it rough by any means necessary. Mel's left hand was slightly squeezing my neck. "Oh, shit. Fuck this pussy harder." I spread my legs wider wanting to feel every inch of his Mandingo.

"Alright, you asked for it," Mel muttered, thrusting all his dick inside of my world, my Earth, whatever you wanted to call it, but his dick was about to cause an earthquake. I didn't know if it was his hands, or his Mandingo, but my volcano was about to explode hot lava all over his dick.

I did ask for it. My hands were sweaty and sliding all over his back as I threw my pussy, matching his thrusts. "This is what you asked for." Mel had both hands around my neck while penetrating inside my world. Within seconds my world came tumbling down, because I creamed all over his dick.

You could call me nasty and I didn't care if it was a quickie, but my mouth was watering. I hopped off the bed, dropped to my knees and inserted his monster dick into my mouth, not giving it a chance to get limp.

"Ahhhhgggghhh!" Mel tried to run from me as I deep throated his dick. I was gagging and trying to take in as much as I could.

I continued spitting on his dick and my juices on his dick made it slide easily down my throat. I could tell he was enjoying my head game, because the nigga was whining like a baby and his knees were trembling like it was a cold winter's night.

"Goddamn, dammit man," he moaned out as my neck, mouth and tongue were in full throttle, sucking the life out of him. The more his knees buckled and his moans turned into groans, that shit had my pussy throbbing. I inserted my left finger inside of my wetness, fingering myself as I sucked Mel's dick in rhythm.

"Hmmmm," I moaned, feeling my juices flowing over my fingers at the same time. My mouth filled up with Mel's juices as he busted in my mouth. I tried to spit that shit out. Mel started to laugh as his cum ran down my lips.

"Damn baby, you a beast with that head game."

I didn't say a word. I just got up and walked off into the bathroom. I looked in the mirror and realized why he was laughing at me. His cum was all over my face, like the 'Got Milk' advertisements. I grabbed a rag and wiped my face. I looked back in the mirror and smiled. One day soon, I'm going to be the next Mrs. Brown.

CHAPTER FIVE

Bianca

I stayed in the hospital for two weeks, and then I was released. I was happy to be out of the hospital, but the minute I entered the house, I started having flashbacks of the events that took place on those steps. I felt my chest tightening up on me. I grabbed my purse and my keys from the key holder and stormed back outside. I still wasn't feeling my best, and probably shouldn't be driving, but I needed to make a run.

I Googled gun shops near me and a few of them popped up. I parked and walked in.

"Good afternoon ma'am. How may I help you?"

"I need something small that can do some damage."

"Well, you're in the right place. Come on over here and see what you like."

I followed the elderly man to the counter. I started to look around and one gun caught my attention. It was the right size and it could fit in my purses.

"Lemme see this one." I pointed to the gun in the safe.

"This right here is a baby .380. It is a nice size for somebody like you, who is looking for something that is not too big, but it still can protect you."

He handed it to me. I took it and started examining the gun. It looked powerful enough to put a couple shots into Mel's ass.

"Ok, I like this. How do I go about getting it?"

"Well, you'll need to fill out this paperwork and give me your ID please. I will run a state background check on you."

I dug into my purse and pulled out my ID. Shit, my background was clean, so I wasn't too worried. About an hour later, I was walking out with more confidence than when I first walked in. I threw the bag on the seat and pulled off. I swear, that nigga better stay the fuck away from me, because there was no way I was going to let him put his hands on me again.

***

I decided to run some bath water. I needed to wash the hospital scent off me and relax in some Epsom Salt for a little bit. I lit some candles and poured myself a glass of wine. I closed my eyes, laid back and relaxed in the tub. The music was playing in the background and I just allowed myself to dream away. I popped my eyes open, thinking I heard something. I jumped out of the tub, grabbed my robe and ran out of the bathroom and into my bedroom. I grabbed my gun from my drawer and slowly walked down the steps. I had my gun aimed, just in case anything popped out at me. I looked around, but did not see anything. I walked through the house and quickly noticed that my back door was wide open. That was strange, I thought as I stood there trying to figure out if I should approach the door, or not. I slowly approached the door. It was dark outside and from what I could see, there was no one there. I quickly slammed the door shut. I stood there for a second, thinking hard. I know damn well, that I did not leave my front door open for the entire time that I was in the hospital. I walked off feeling disgusted. I had no idea what was going on, but whatever it was, had me on the edge.

I made one more walk through, checking the garage and making sure all my windows were closed. I got upstairs and dialed Lexi's number. I hadn't spoken to her in a few days and needed someone to talk to. Plus, I needed to know how the shop was going.

"Hey chick. Are you still at the hospital?"

"No, I'm home. I think Mel was trying to spook me right now."

"What do you mean, trying to spook you?

"I was taking a bath and I thought I heard something, I got out of the tub and went downstairs. That's when I realized my back door was wide open. I looked around and didn't see anyone, but I know I didn't leave it open."

"He still lives there, right? So, he probably just forgot to lock the door."

"He shouldn't be here. Not when the police are looking for him. Tomorrow I'm going to get a restraining order against him. I want him out of my life for good."

"Calm down Bianca. You need to think all of this through before you do something that might hurt you in the end."

"Think about it? Girl, that's all I did when I was in that hospital room with a banged-up face. I hate that nigga and everything that he stands for. Soon as my kids come back home, I'm thinking about getting

46

the fuck outta this state and as far as I can get away from him."

"I mean, you're grown and all, but as your friend, I just want you to do what's best for you and them babies."

"Listen, I know it's late, so let me get off this phone… Oh Lexi, one more thing."

"What's up?"

"You haven't been telling Mel anything we talk about, right?"

"Hell nah! Why would you ask me such a thing? I mean, I like Mel and all, but you my bitch and I would never betray you like that."

"I'm sorry Lexi. It's just that Mel said something to me when he was beating on me and I was wondering how the fuck he knew about that? Anyway, let me go. We will talk tomorrow."

DEVOTED TO A STREET KING

I hung the phone up and sat at the edge of the bed with the gun close by. I was tired mentally and physically and needed to get some rest. Tomorrow was a new day and I had some serious decisions to make.

***

The next day I Googled locksmiths. I didn't trust Mel, and needed to change the locks immediately. I found a company and chose to call them after reading the reviews. I told the guy that I spoke to on the phone that I needed it done that day. He understood and made the appointment for three pm.

I sat in the living room waiting for the locksmith. He was on the way over to change the locks for me and then I was going to change the code on the alarm system. I heard the doorbell ring and jumped up. I popped the door open and my mouth dropped open. "Good morning ma'am. You want to change the locks on your doors?"

It was only when I heard his sexy, sultry voice that I picked my lip up. I was embarrassed that I was behaving like a young school girl.

"Yes, that would be me. Come in Jarvis," I said after reading his name on his name tag.

"I want all the locks changed please. I also want a dead bolt on the back door."

He proceeded to work and I went back into the living room, pretending like I was reading a magazine. When I tell you that man was easy on the eyes, he was and his muscles were screaming grab me through his work shirt. I wondered where his woman was, because if he was my man, he would not be walking around so freely. A little voice in my head quickly warned me to stop the foolishness. The last thing I needed to be thinking about was a man. I just got beat down by a nigga that I once fell head over heels for.

"Mrs. Brown, I am finished. Do you want to keep these old locks?"

"No, I don't, but how can I keep you?" I joked, but was shocked that I had the nerve to say it.

"Hah, ha. That's the nicest thing a customer has ever said to me."

"Well, do you have a woman?"

"No ma'am. I'm single."

"Drop the ma'am. My name is Bianca."

"Well in that case, hello Bianca." He took my hand and kissed it.

Call me a whore, but shit, I wanted to just tackle him to the floor and ride his dick.

"I know you're working, but I can sure use a cup of tea. What about you?"

"I finished early, so I do have a little time to chill before my next appointment."

He sat at the kitchen table while we got acquainted. That man's mind was a force to be reckoned with. I sat across from him, hanging on to every word that flew out of his mouth. Not only was he stimulating my mind, but my pussy was being stimulated with moisture. I guess he felt the same way, because he got up and without warning, he picked me up from the stool. He carried me to the living room and laid me on the couch. My brain was telling me to get the fuck up, but I ignored that shit, closed my eyes and braced myself for whatever nastiness that man was about to do to me.

I felt no guilt on the inside. I just needed to be held tight and fucked right. Jarvis wasted no time slipping my gown over my head. He stared at my body, shaking his head with disbelief. "Hmmm, hmmm," he moaned before cupping my breasts and sucking on my nipples.

"Aweee, aweee," I squealed when his sexy LL Cool J lips kissed my nipple. I swear, right then I

51

wanted to melt into pieces. "Oh yessss!" I caressed the back of his head. His lips felt like they belonged on my body by the way he made me twitch.

After kissing my other nipple, he ran his tongue down my stomach and then started licking and sucking on my naval. I pushed his head between my legs. My pussy was doing the two-step dance, wanting some attention. At least that was what I thought it was doing, because my body back peddled until I fell onto the couch.

My legs were bent behind the couch arm, which gave Jarvis access between my legs. He folded my legs up and his tongue found its way to my pretty pearl.

"Hmmm." I closed my eyes letting him have his way with my body. His tongue made my body shiver each time he licked my insides. "Oh, my goodness." I don't know what he was doing to me, but I loved it.

His tongue was plunging in and out of my pussy. Grinding my hips in rhythm with my hands still locked around his head, I guided him in and out of my pussy.

"Oh, my goodness! Oh shit, Sssss, I'm cumming," I moaned out in ecstasy as my juices traveled down my legs.

"Damn, that felt so good." I had to admit his tongue did the trick, but I wondered what his dick game was about. I was feeling naughty. "Let's get it on daddy." I stood up and bent over the arm of the couch with my feet on the floor and my midsection on the couch. In that position, it was clear that I watched too many porn movies.

"Let's get it in ma." Jarvis's mushroom shaped dick entered my wet warm pussy with ease. "Damn, this shit feels so good." He placed his hands on my lower back as his dick penetrated in and out my pussy, driving me insane.

"Shit yes! It's your pussy!" I yelled out feeling good as his nuts started slapping my ass. He kept slapping my ass, causing it to bounce more. "Yes, daddy fuck me!" I didn't know if I was feeling myself, but his dick was so deep inside of me. I wanted to tap out, but I had asked for it. I had to be careful what I asked for.

"Oh shit, oh shit," he groaned, speeding up his thrusts. I tried to throw my pussy back at him the best way possible, but I was in an awkward position.

"Oh shit," he continued to groan as sweat poured down his face. My juices flowed through my body once again, and I found myself cumming on his dick.

We came at the same time, but I wasn't about to let that good dick fucker get away. "They say the third time's a charm," I said ready to bust nut number three. Jarvis was sitting up on the couch with his dick semi limp. I got on my knees and wrapped my lips around his dick, sucking it back to everlasting life. It only took four hard pulls with my month before he was ready for action.

I eased myself on his dick backwards and braced my hands on the table, so my ass could be tooted and spread as wide as possible. His hands were on my waist guiding me up and down on his dick. "Ooooh, baby," I heard him sing out while my ass jiggled on his dick.

Oh, my goodness, I was feeling his dick in my stomach, tapping a few tubes. I continued making my ass clap on his dick. Sweat beads formed on my head as I sped up my pace. My adrenaline was pumping hard and my juices were leaking between my legs as I reached my climax.

I swear that man almost ripped my insides out, but as much as it hurt, it felt just as good.

"That was some good pussy," the once well-mannered man said.

"That dick of yours was good as hell too." I winked at him.

I wanted to move, but I was feeling tired as hell. "Damn, look at the time. I got to run. Can I wash up in your bathroom really quick?"

"Of course, let me grab you a washcloth and a towel."

I got up, grabbed my clothes and put them on.

"Come on, follow me." I walked up the stairs.

"The bathroom is right there."

While he was washing up, I was still trying to justify what I'd just done. I mean, I'd never given the pussy up to a man that I didn't know. Shit, I was happy he had a condom, because God knows that nigga could've had HIV and I didn't know.

He walked out of the bathroom fully dressed.

"Aye, I'm about to bounce, but I want to know if that was just a one fuck, or can I see you again?"

"Well, you got my number, so call me when you're free."

"A'ight bet. By the way, that bill is on me."

"No way. I don't want your boss to get on your ass about his money."

"Well, since I'm the boss, you ain't got anything to worry about." He winked at me, smiled and walked down the stairs.

I tried to say something, but no words came out. I guess he told my ass. I waited for him to walk out the door, then I walked over and locked the door. I was happy that the locks were changed and I didn't have to worry about Mel bringing his ass up in there.

I decided to take a quick shower, because my pussy was sore and I needed the cold water to soothe it a little.

CHAPTER SIX

Lexi

I was happy to finally be off work. It was a long day and it made it worse that I had to take on Bianca's clients also. I'd be happy when that bitch got better, so she could handle her own damn business. Shit, the only thing I wanted to handle was her damn husband. Speaking of Mel, I hadn't heard from him all day. Matter of fact, he should've been at the house. I climbed the stairs and checked to see if he was home, but he wasn't. I grabbed my cell phone from my purse and dialed his number. His phone rang until his voicemail came on. That was strange, because he always answered his phone whenever I called. I started panicking, wondering if the police had his ass. I browsed the internet for the county jail and dialed the number.

"DeKalb County City Jail. How may I help you?"

"Yes, hello, I'm trying to see if y'all have an inmate named Melvin Brown."

"Hold on…"

My heart was racing and my palms were sweaty. I swear, this was not how I planned my life with him. I wanted happiness, not a nigga who was going to be in and out of jail. Shit, I did that in my twenties and damn sure wasn't about to be in and out of a visitation room.

"Ma'am, we don't have anyone by that name here."

I hung up instantly and let out a long sigh, but that didn't last. If he was not locked up, where the fuck was he and why was that nigga not answering his phone? All kind of ideas popped in my head. I jumped up, grabbed my phone and my keys and headed out the door.

I pulled up at Bianca's house. I wanted to see if he was back over there. I parked across the street and watched her house. I continuously dialed his number, but the voicemail was the only thing I kept getting. I noticed that a car pulled into her driveway. I popped my head up a little to see if it was Mel, but that dude was tall and built with hair. I wondered who the fuck he was? I was curious to find out, but was also careful not to get noticed. I watched as Bianca came to the door. They hugged and if I wasn't mistaken, I could've sworn I saw them kiss before he walked in the house. She looked around, then walked back in the house, closing the door behind her.

I thought about going up and ringing the doorbell. I was so damn nosey, but there was no way I could explain what I was doing at her house that time of night. I started my car up and slowly pulled off. My mind quickly went back to the situation at hand. Where the fuck was Mel? Shit, his wife was creeping with some other nigga and he was nowhere to be found.

I heard my phone ringing. At first I ignored it, but it continued ringing. I opened my eyes and noticed it was morning already. Fuck! I jumped up and grabbed the phone. Damn, I thought, when I noticed it was my client that I was supposed to go meet at eight am. "Good morning Miss Sadie."

"I been ringing the bell, are you inside there?"

"No ma'am, I am so sorry. I wasn't feeling too good and was at the emergency room all night," I lied.

"Oh, no dear. Are you doing ok?"

"Not really. I think I came down with one of those 24 hour bugs."

"Sorry to hear. You know what? Let's just reschedule for whenever you feel better."

"Are you sure? Because I can still come get you done."

"Yes, I'm sure. Get you some rest and drink plenty water. The weather is changing, so a lot of that's going around."

"Alright then, Miss Sadie. I will give you a call as soon as I feel better."

I hung up the phone and felt relieved. It was Monday, but I did not plan on going in. Shit, Bianca ass was out whoring around, so she damn sure could go to work and run her shit.

I was just about to go upstairs when I heard my front door opening. I stopped and waited because I knew only one person had keys to my place.

"Hey babe." That nigga walked in smiling.

"Really Melvin? You been gone for how long and just walk up in here smiling and shit. Where the fuck you been?"

"Where the fuck I been? Damn you sound like Bianca's ass. I was with the fellas shooting pool and I was too drunk to drive home."

"First off, please don't ever compare me to your bitch. That shit might fly with her, but not me. I know how you are and what you're capable of doing. Don't forget, we've been creeping around for over a year, so I know you a fucking dog," I lashed out.

"You need to chill out and stop acting like you the Virgin Mary. You just as at fault as I am. Shit, she's your friend, but that did not stop you from letting me slide up in them drawers."

"Really Mel? That's how you feel about me? I didn't put a gun to your head. You could've walked away if I wasn't what you wanted. But no, you stayed promising me that you're going to get a divorce, and now we got a baby on the way. But nigga that is beside the point. Where the fuck you been?"

"I told you, I was with the fellas. Listen up, if I wanted to be treated like a little boy and hear constant bitching, I would've stayed with that bitch over there. I told you, I hate a nagging ass female. If you want us to be together, you need to tighten the fuck up shawty, or we can go our separate ways. I will still help you with my child."

By the time, he was finished talking, tears were rolling down my face. I had never seen that side of Mel before. Shit, he had never raised his voice at me before, but there he was talking to me like I was beneath me.

"You know what Mel, I know you probably back creeping with Bianca's ass, but the joke is really on you, 'cause Bianca got a new nigga sleeping in the same bed, y'all slept in. You put that bitch on a pedestal, but guess what? That hoe ain't no better than the rest of us."

His eyes widened and the veins in his forehead popped open. "What the fuck you talking about? What nigga Bianca had over there?" His voice trembled.

"Wow! You that angry over a bitch that you claim you don't give a fuck about? Nigga you're a fucking joke, for real."

He walked over to me, grabbed my shoulder and started shaking me.

"Tell me, what nigga Bianca had at the house!"

"Get the fuck off me, first of all." I tried to push him off. "Next, if you so curious, go find out for yourself. Shit, you got that bitch's number, or matter of fact, you still have her fucking keys. So, how about you run your little ass over there and see for your damn self." The tears continued flowing like a river.

He took several steps towards me and grabbed me up in a bear hug. "Baby calm down. This ain't good for you and my baby. I love you, not her, or no other bitch for that matter. I fucking need you in my life. Don't turn your back on me now babe."

I wanted to say fuck him, but the truth was, I loved that man. I didn't want to act like the other bitches he had dealt with before. I wanted to be his calm during all the storms that he was dealing with in his life. I wanted him to be around to help raise our baby.

I held on to him and just let the tears flow. "I love you too Melvin. I swear I do."

We must've stood there a good fifteen minute just professing our love for each other. Afterwards, I cooked him breakfast, we ate and then bathed together. Being with him made me totally forget how I was feeling about him earlier. I swear, I could really get used to the situation.

I heard my cellphone ringing. I didn't want to move from the comfort of his arms and answer the damn phone, but it continued ringing.

I looked at that caller ID and realized it was Bianca. Fuck, what the hell did that bitch want?

"Be quiet. It's your wife," I whispered to him before I answered.

"Hello."

"Hey Lexi. I thought you was at the shop. I just got here and the shop is closed."

"Oh hey, I'm sorry I forgot to call you. I don't feel too hot today. It might've been something that I ate. I got diarrhea really bad."

"Oh ok, I'm sorry to hear that. I wish you had called me. I could've came in earlier, but no worries. I will stop by and check on you later."

"Bianca, thanks boo, but I feel so sick. I'm just gonna crawl up in the bed and sleep. I should feel better by tomorrow and I definitely will be there bright and early."

"Alright, well get some rest then. If you need me, just holla. I got some heads to do, so I will be here most of the day."

"A'ight babes."

Mel turned around and looked at me. "What the hell she wanted?"

"Just checking to see why I didn't come in."

"Did she say anything about me?"

"Nah Mel, she didn't mention you. I told you she moved on with that other nigga. Now you can get your divorce and we can move on with our lives."

I was waiting on a response, but never got one. Instead, he rolled back over and within minutes that nigga was fast asleep. I knew what he said earlier, but I swear I knew he lying. That nigga might not be in love with her, but he damn sure didn't want no other nigga over there.

My plan was to make him totally forget about that bitch. I didn't know how I was going to do it, but I planned on it. I laid on the bed, looking up at the ceiling and thinking of my next move.

CHAPTER SEVEN

Bianca

Hmm, after I got off the phone, with Lexi, I was feeling some type of way. How the fuck was she was supposed to open the shop today and she didn't? I loved her to death, but lately her behavior was becoming ridiculous. I knew we were friends and shit, but business was business and when my money started looking funny, then it became an issue. Tomorrow, I planned on addressing the situation, because if she was too busy to handle her duties, I had no problem replacing her.

I heard the door open and I stood up, quickly noticing that it was the detective who was working on my case. I knew he called and left me a message, but the truth was, I forgot to call him back.

"Hello Detective Salmon."

"Hello Mrs. Brown."

"I see you're back at work. How you feeling?"

"I'm doing better. Still feeling a little bit of pain." I smiled.

"Well, I must tell you, you look much better. Have your husband contacted you?"

"No, I haven't seen him since that night. However, I think he was in my house the night I came home from the hospital."

"Well, we've been looking for him, but still can't seem to catch up with him. Do you know any particular place he may be hiding out at?"

"No, not at all. I know his family lives in upstate NY, but I doubt he would run up there to them. He hasn't been in contact with them."

"Well, you need to be aware of your surroundings while he's still at large. You might want to get some pepper spray, or something and call us if you see him before we do."

"Ok Detective. Thank you."

"Enjoy the rest of your day ma'am."

He walked out and I went back to doing what I was doing. It was strange that Mel, has not been arrested yet. I mean, I did not know of any place that he could be hiding, but then again, his ass could be shacked up with the bitch that he was cheating on me with. I couldn't help but wonder who the fuck that bitch was. Oh well, he was her problem now, because as soon as I got some time, I planned on filing for a divorce.

The biggest task was telling the kids that mommy and daddy were no longer together. I knew I might have to take them to counseling, because the truth was, although he was a horrible husband, he was a good father to his children. I didn't plan on taking them out of his life, I would never hurt my kids that way.

Oh, what a day, I thought as I set the alarm at the salon and walked to my car. I'd been on my damn feet all damn day. I'd done three quick weaves, two sew in and a few wash and sets. It didn't help any that Lexi didn't come in either.

My phone started ringing and I pulled it out of my purse. I saw that it was Jarvis. My face lit up as I answered the phone. "Hey you."

"Hey beautiful. How you doing?"

"Tired as hell. Just leaving the shop."

"Damn, I was just going to invite you out to dinner. I know this nice little Italian restaurant downtown that has a live band on Monday nights. Since you just got off work, I'm going to grab takeout from Red Lobster. I will be over shortly."

"Ok, see you in a few."

I was so damn tired. It was one of those nights that I could do without company. I was falling fast and hard for Jarvis, however, I was careful. I was still married to that asshole and I didn't want to bring him into my drama. I knew he a little younger than me, but trust me, that nigga did not carry himself that way. The dick was on point, he ate pussy good, he made his own money and most importantly, he respected me. I mean, at the time that was all I needed.

I took a quick shower when I got home and put on a nice little dress that showed my cleavage and my ass. I walked downstairs to sit in the living room and waited on him. Five minutes later, I heard the doorbell ringing. I knew it was him, so I wasted no time. I got up, dashed to the door and opened it. He was standing there with his sexy self with that NY fitted cap on. That athletic outfit had him looking extra sexy tonight. I had to take my eyes off him quickly and try to get my thoughts together. I was no sex fiend, but sex was the first thing on my mind whenever I was in his presence.

"Hey babe." He gave me a hug and walked past me with his hand filled with bags full of food. I saw a bottle of wine too.

"Hey you. What you got in those bags? I'm famished."

"Well, I didn't know what you wanted. So, I got a little of e'erything. Fish, shrimp, wings, steak. Come see for yourself."

"Damn dude, you acting like you was about to feed the entire neighborhood," I busted out laughing.

I grabbed two glass from the cabinet and popped the wine bottle open. I poured a glass for him and myself. He lit the candles that were on the table. I swear, it was nothing major, but the setting was very romantic. I'd been married to a jerk for so long that I failed to realize how a woman was supposed to be treated.

"So, how was your day babe?"

"Well, mine was pretty easy. I only had three security systems to install today. So, the rest of the day, I just hit the gym. I thought about dropping by the shop to see my babe, but I didn't want to get your coworkers in your business."

"Shit, you should've came. I was there by myself. My right hand didn't bother to show up and the other chick is on maternity leave. When I tell you that I worked like I was the damn helper, please believe me."

"Damn, well eat up so I can run your bath water. I'm going to bathe you and massage your tired body."

"Well, in that case, let me shut the fuck up and eat. 'Cause baby, my body needs a well-deserved massage." I laughed.

We continued eating, drinking wine and just enjoying each other's company. "Let me ask you a question Jarvis."

"What's up babe?"

"What do you want from me?"

He put his fork down and rubbed his hands together. "Well, let's see. I ain't about to sit here and feed you no lies. When we first started out, all I wanted to do was fuck. I mean, let's be real, look at how we met? But the more time we spend together, the stronger my feelings are becoming. I 'ont want to sound mushy, or no shit like that, but shawty I'm digging you. I want you. I want more out of this…"

"You do know I'm still married and I have kids. I mean, I'm going to get a divorce, but the kids are forever."

"Shit, I love kids. I don't have any of my own, but I have nieces and nephews and they all love me. I don't mind you having kids. I accepted your kids the minute I started dating you."

I was smiling inside, because this dude was just so different. I knew he could be running game on me, but for the moment, I was enjoying the feeling he was giving me.

After dinner, he helped me clean the kitchen up. Then he ran my bath water and bathed me from head to toe, while slow music played in the background. I swear I could get used to this. When he was finished, he carried me to the room.

"Lay on your stomach." He started massaging me down with body oil. His hands manhandled my body in a good way, especially when he massaged my ass gently. My pussy started to pay attention to him. I laid there hoping he would hurry the fuck up and turn me on my back. God must've heard my prayer, because he flipped me over and started massaging my breasts and then down my middle. He gently slid a finger inside of my already wet pussy.

"Damn babe, you already wet," he whispered in my ear.

He then slowly buried his head between my legs, first nibbling on my clit. He raised my legs over his shoulders while he feasted on my pussy. "Awee damn babe!" I screamed out as he latched on to my clit.

"Yo', you whore! Who is this nigga you have in my bed?" I heard a familiar voice ask.

Jarvis jumped up and I also jumped off the bed. I didn't need to hear that voice again to know who the fuck it was. I wasted no time opening my drawer to grab my gun. By then Jarvis and Mel was on the ground scuffling. I could see that Jarvis had his ass and as much as I wanted to enjoy the moment, I was too caught up in trying to dial 911. I walked into the bathroom and let the dispatcher know that a wanted man was in my house.

"Jarvis, baby, get off him. The police are on the way." I grabbed Jarvis by the shirt and tried to pull him up.

"You bitch! This is my motherfucking house. You have the fucking nerve to bring a bum ass nigga up in here." He lunged toward me.

"You better back the fuck up before I blow your brains all over this fucking floor." I pointed the gun at him. Jarvis was ready to beat his ass again, but I stopped him. I knew the police were on the way.

I heard somebody banging on the door. Mel heard it also, and tried to dash to the stairs. I wasn't worried, because I knew they had the house surrounded. He ran downstairs into the garage and I hurriedly opened the door.

"Officer, he just ran into the garage, so he should be coming out on the side." A couple officers dashed to the side while two came into the house to search.

"Put your hands up!" I heard an officer yell.

"We got him. We got him."

I heard a tussle and then a few minutes later, they walked Mel toward the front in handcuffs. His face was all bruised up from fighting with Jarvis and the police.

He looked at me as they walked him by me.

"You gonna pay for this Bianca. I ain't did shit to you."

I did not respond. Instead, I just turned to walk away. I saw Jarvis talking to the police, so I walked over to check on my boo. "You good?"

"Yeah, how about you?"

"If you're good, I'm good."

I talked to the officer for a few minutes and then we walked back into the house. That was when it hit me. I'd changed my locks, but he still had the garage opener on his car. How could I be so careless? Hmm, I needed to tighten up because Jarvis and I could've lost our lives behind that fool.

Soon as we got back inside, I poured myself a glass of wine. That shit was fucking crazy. That nigga tried it. I noticed Jarvis sitting there in silence. I placed the glass on the table and knelt in front of him. I took his hands and stared into his eyes.

"Listen babe. I am sorry about what happened tonight. I didn't mean to pull you into my craziness, so if you want to fall back from this, I understand."

"Bianca, cut that bullshit out. I'm a man and I know what the fuck I want. That cat ain't did shit to sway me away from you. I'm kinda mad that you didn't let me rearrange his face the way I wanted to though. But other that, you good. I want you and there is no way anyone is gonna stop me from getting to you."

A bitch was feeling kind of emotional. I didn't know where we were headed, but I was ready to ride it out with him.

"Come on, let's go back to bed." I grabbed his hand and we walked upstairs hand in hand.

CHAPTER EIGHT

Lexi

Mel said he was running to the store and was supposed to be coming right back. That was two hours ago. There we go with the bullshit. I didn't know how many times I would have to deal with him and his disappearing acts. I grabbed my phone and dialed his number. There was no answer and his voicemail came on.

I sent him a text.

Really Mel? This is what we're doing again?

I waited for a response, but I did not get one. I texted him again, but still no response. I sat there in disbelief that he was on his bullshit again.

I walked downstairs, and grabbed the bottle of Crown Royal. I poured a glass, and sat on the couch and swallowed the liquor in big gulps. Before I could put the glass down, I heard my cellphone ringing. I rushed upstairs and grabbed the phone without paying any attention to the caller ID. "You have a collect call from, Melvin Brown, an inmate at DeKalb County Jail. Press one to accept the call and 5 to ignore this call."

My heart sank, as I tried to grip an understanding of what was really taking place. I pressed one to accept the call and braced myself.

"Yo' baby, I'm glad you picked up the phone."

"What the fuck happened? And what are you charged with?"

"Man, they picked me up because of that bitch. I swear I'ma kill that hoe when I get out of here man…"

"You need to shut the hell up, talking like that. You do know all phone calls are recorded, right?"

"Man, I'm heated as fuck and don't give a damn who the fuck is listening to me right about now."

I could see that I wasn't getting anywhere with him, so I switched up the subject.

"Do you have a bond?"

"Yea, that shit $30,000 and you got to pay 10% of it. Damn baby, if you pay the bond, I will pay you back soon as I get out."

"A'ight, I don't even know where to look for a bondsman. Hmm, let me jump on line and see. Just sit tight."

"Lexi, baby. You know I love you, right? I'm kind of happy this happened, because now I can get a divorce from that bitch and you and I can make it official, if you know what I mean."

"Alright Mel. Let's try to get you out of there first. Then we can talk about that other shit."

"You right boo. I will be sitting tight."

"Alright. Love you, and I'll see you in a little while."

I hung the phone up feeling relieved. I was happy that he wasn't with another bitch like I thought. I jumped on line and started looking for a BAIL BONDSMAN near me.

I thought about leaving his ass in there to let his wife, deal with him, but who was I fooling. I was in love with that man and it was my chance to prove to him that I was a better woman than his wife. There was no way I would've called the police on him and I would not get him arrested.

***

I stood anxiously waiting on him to come out. I felt like a young girl, waiting for the ice cream truck. I spotted him walking out, dashed over to him and jumped in his arms. "HEY BABYYYY!" I yelled.

"Damn, you happy to see daddy, ain't you" He cuffed my ass through the leggings that I was wearing. "Don't you start no shit, or I'll have to fuck you out here in this parking lot," I whispered.

"Damn, my dick's hard already. Come on, let's get out of here."

We walked out of the county jail, hand in hand. We got in the car and I pulled off. I was happy to have my man back, but he was angry. The entire ride, he kept rambling on and on about Bianca and how he was going to make her pay.

"Damn baby, let it go. You just need to find you a lawyer and deal with her in court. If not, you gonna fuck around and lose everything."

He wasn't letting up about what he was going to do to her. I turned the music up, trying to drown his rambling out a little. There was no way I was going to say I do to him with that bitch weighing heavily on his mind.

"Did that bitch say anything to you about me getting locked up?" He hollered over the music.

"No, I haven't spoken to her. I'll see her at work in the am. I'm pretty sure she can't wait to tell me all about it."

"Baby listen, you can't start believing shit that comes out of that bitch's mouth. Remember, she's a scorned bitch that will do, or say anything to hold on to me. You can't let her lies get in your head."

"Mel, you must think I'm some young, dumb bitch. I'm a grown bitch and there's nothing a hoe can tell me to convince me that you did something to her. When Bianca be talking, I just be sitting there looking at her. Deep inside, I be like, if only that bitch knew."

"Ok, good. I knew you wasn't the average woman. I love you babe."

"I love you too."

***

After we got him home, I fucked and sucked him properly. Then I decided to take him to Buffalo Wild Wings, so we could grab a bite to eat. Their food was off the chain, plus it was Tuesday and they had drinks for two dollars. I couldn't drink, but Mel sure could use a couple drinks. My goal was to get him out of the funk that he was in.

Soon as we were seated, he started back on his rampage. "Yo, that bitch can't get my kids," he said in a serious tone.

"Well, be ready to fight, because you know damn well, Bianca is nasty. She's not gonna just give in and let her kids go. Furthermore, you got a baby on the way to worry about."

"Yeah, I know boo, but I want all my damn kids to grow up together. Plus, I don't want my fucking kids around that punk ass young nigga she fucking."

My antenna went up instantly and I turned my attention to him fully. How the fuck did he know who she was fucking? I told him it was a nigga, but not once did I mention a young nigga.

"Wait, how do you know the dude she's fucking is young? Have you met him?" I shot him a suspicious look.

"Nah I ain't met him. I just know Bianca and I know she love fucking around wit' them young ass niggas that still got breast milk on their breath."

"Oh ok…" I said, although I didn't believe a word that was coming out of his mouth.

"Good evening and welcome to Buffalo Wild Wings. Can I take your order?" The waitress walked to the table and interrupted my thoughts.

After we ordered our food, Mel switched up the conversation fast.

"Aye, we need to go to the bank in the morning, so I can pay you back that money. We need to grab some baby stuff tomorrow too. Time is flying, but I'm so ready to meet my baby."

See, that nigga was no fool. He knew how to soften my heart. I knew he had other kids, but fuck that. My baby was going to be number one in his life. Trust me, mama was going to make sure of that.

"You good babe?"

"Oh yeah...Sorry, I'm good. Just got a little carried away thinking about our baby."

He reached across the table and grabbed my hand. "Babe, I promise e'erything gonna be a'ight. Just trust your man."

"I know boo." I squeezed his hand.

Our food came and we sat in complete silence. We were both caught up in our own feelings. I would pay money to know what was going on in his mind. Was he thinking about me and the baby, or was he worried about that bitch and her bastards?

After we finished eating, I called the waitress over and paid her. I also left a tip and we got up to leave. "Damn babe, it's kind of chilly out there," he said as he placed his arm around me. We were about to exit the building when my eyes popped open.

"Lexi girl, how you doing?" A big mouthed bitch named Charlay stopped us in our tracks.

"Hey chick. Long time no see. How you doing?" I barely asked, not giving a fuck. I didn't care for her ass.

"You know me, I'm always on my grind. Trying to get it how I live. By the way, congrats on the new bundle. I know how hard it was for you to get pregnant. By the way, you not goin' introduce me to the handsome man?"

"Oh yeah..." I was frozen.

"Wait...your face looks familiar. Have we met before?" She turned her attention to Mel.

"No, we've never met and I'm pretty good with faces."

"Hmmm, well they say we all have a double out there. Well, my name is Charlay, nice to meet you."

"Hello Charlay. It's my pleasure."

"Well Charlay, it's getting late and we got to run."

"A'ight girl. My number's still the same, so hit me up sometimes."

"Alrighty."

I was happy to finally step out the door and out into some fresh air. It was like I was suffocating while I was standing there talking to that bitch. I knew exactly where she remembered Mel from. She was there when we had our grand opening at the shop. I wouldn't put it past the bitch that she remembered him and was only playing crazy.

"Babe, where you know that chick from? You didn't seem too happy to see her."

"You don't remember her? She was at our grand opening at the shop. I think she and Bianca went to hair school together."

"Damn! Do you think she remembers me?" He sounded concerned.

"Why the fuck you so fucking worried? I mean, how long you think we are gonna hide this from Bianca. My baby is due in two more months and I don't plan on hiding shit when my baby gets here!" I lashed out.

"Damn Lexi, what the fuck you so worried about? I told yo' ass I love you and I want to be with you. Trust me, if I wanted to be with that bitch, I would be wit' her ass, not here with you and my seed."

I didn't bother to respond, because I saw that nigga was on the edge. Even though he said he did not beat Bianca up, I knew damn well he did it and I swear, I did not want to become his next victim. We got in the car and I pulled off.

We got home and got in the bed. We didn't say much to each other and I was cool with that, because I needed him. There was no way I was going to put up with all his bullshit though. I browsed on Facebook until my eyes started getting blurry. I logged off, turned my back to him and tried to doze off. I was awakened out of my sleep because of the ringing of a phone. I snatched up mine off the nightstand, but quickly realized that it wasn't my phone, but his.

"Yo', your phone is ringing." I shook him, but he did not flinch. I guess that nigga was dead to the world. I laid my head back down on the pillow, but that damn phone wasn't easing up at all. I glanced at my phone and realized that it was a little after one am. So, who the fuck would be calling that nigga's phone like that? Shit, he had two phones. One of them was for him to deal with the streets and the other one was his personal phone. I was sure it was the personal one that was ringing because he had, "Ran Off On The Plug" by Plies as his ringtone. I looked over at him. He was still in a deep sleep, snoring and all. I took my time, eased up from the bed and tiptoed around to his side of the bed. I got low on the floor and crawled to where his pants were. I was nervous, but that didn't stop me from pulling his pants towards me. I then crept to the bathroom. I closed the bathroom door, hoping that he would stay sleep. I looked at the phone and it was ten missed calls from a number that was not saved with a name. Hmmm, I started thinking. I clicked on his text messages. God, I was not prepared for what I was about to read. Some bitch texted him, talking about she was missing him and couldn't wait to see him. I guess that was the bitch that was calling nonstop. Another bitch texted that she needed milk and pampers for their daughter. I clutched my chest as I continued reading. After reading text messages from about six bitches, I was so done. I sat on the toilet seat with tears rolling down my face. That nigga was fucking cheating with all those bitches. Not just that, but that nigga had another baby out there. Ohhhh, my God, what had I gotten myself into? I cried silently and then looked down, realizing that I was still clutching his phone. I eased myself up and wiped the snot from my running nose. I walked out of the bathroom and threw his pants on the floor. He jumped up, looking startled.

"Yo', what the fuck? You a'ight?" That bastard sat up in the bed looking all crazy and shit.

"Yes, I'm good. Trust me." I then walked out of the room and down the stairs. God, I was beating myself up for being a fucking fool. I thought I was the only one he was fucking with after he left Bianca, but no, that nigga was slinging dick everywhere he could. I felt a sharp pain in my stomach. I tried to make my way to the kitchen to make a cup of tea, but I stumbled and fell. "Mellllll!" I screamed with the little energy I had in me.

I was panicking as flashbacks of my past miscarriages flashed in my mind. I started feeling dizzy.

"Oh, my God baby, what's wrong?"

"Call the ambulance please," I barely got out.

"Nah fuck that. I'm driving you to the hospital."

"God please, don't let me lose this baby," I whispered to myself.

"Hang on babe. Hang on. I got you." He picked me up and carried me to the couch.

I was in extreme pain and couldn't stop the tears from flowing. "Please, hurry up." I was pleading my heart out.

He ran back into the living room, picked me up and carried me out to the car. I was still in night clothes, but that was the least of my worries. On the way to the hospital, all I could think about was losing my baby.

"I need a doctor now!" he screamed out as he ran through the hospital door.

The security and some people in scrubs ran over to us. "What is the problem sir?"

"She is seven months pregnant and she collapsed on the floor."

"Get me a gurney and a doctor!" the nurse yelled.

Everyone rushed toward me and they took me to the back. I was instantly hooked up to an IV and the doctor came in. After examining me, they ordered me to go to the Labor and Delivery Ward, because I was going into labor. It was then that my heart started hurting more. I was only seven months pregnant and had two more months to go.

I was later informed that my water broke and they had to induce my labor. All along Mel was right there with me, asking questions and seeming very concerned. I was still angry, at him, but for the time being, I tried to lower my blood pressure because my baby was in distress and I needed to calm down.

After a long and tiring twelve hours, my baby girl entered the world. I was too tired and weak to take part in the celebration, but please believe it, I was happy as hell. She was placed in the incubator, because she was born with jaundice and was barely four pounds.

After I was cleaned up, and the doctors and nurses were out of the room, Mel walked up to me, grabbed my hand and kissed me on the forehead. "Damn, you did it babe. You did it."

I wanted to address the shit that I saw earlier, but the energy wasn't there and I wasn't going to bring any drama on the day that I was most happy.

"Babe listen to me, I swear I am going to love and take care of you and our daughter for the rest of y'all lives. Matter of fact, yo' ass ain't got to go back to that shop. Soon as you feeling better, find yo' own shop, so you can run yo' own shit."

That was music to my ears, because God knows shit was about to hit the fan and I was not prepared to deal with Bianca and her old dramatic ass.

"Well babe, I need to make a few runs. I will be back up here in a few hours to see you and my daughter." He kissed me on the forehead.

He didn't wait for me to say anything. He was gone in a split second. It took me a few minutes to gather my thoughts. I was a now a mom after all those years of struggling and having miscarriages. There I was finally with the love of my life, little Miss Diamond Brown. Yes, my baby did get her daddy's last name, because there was no other way it was going to be done.

I heard my phone ringing, so I reached over and grabbed it. It was Bianca. Shit, what the fuck did she want at that moment. "Hey girl."

"Damn, that's how you do? I had to hear through the grapevine that you had my God baby? Bitch, when did we become strangers?"

I took a few seconds to think about how I was going to respond. "Bianca chill out, this ain't about you honey. I was at home. I didn't feel good and I thought I was just tired. I went into the kitchen to make me a cup of tea, but I got weak and fell out."

"Damn, I'm so sorry. Is the baby ok?"

"Yes, she is beautiful. You should see her," I gloated.

"I can imagine. Well, I got two more heads to wrap up and then I'ma shoot by there to see you."

My heart dropped when she said that, because Mel was about to come back up there a little later. Lord, I was in no physical shape to be whooping that bitch's ass.

CHAPTER NINE

Bianca

I was tired as fuck, but I promised Lexi that I would swing by the hospital to check on her and my God baby. I had picked up some stuff for the baby, but there was no way I was going to stop at home and then go to the hospital. I would just take it to her once she was released from the hospital.

I parked and dragged myself into the hospital. After I got her room number, I pressed the button for the elevator and waited. I knocked on the door before I entered. Bianca's eyes were closed, so I slowly tapped her leg.

She opened her eyes. "Hey chick." She smiled.

"How you doing?"

"I'm good. A little bit sore, but seeing my princess's face makes it all worth it, you know?"

"Girl, I am so damn happy for you. I know how much you wanted this and I know you will be a great mother. By the way, where is the Mr. at? He was here, right?"

"Huh?" She acted like she did not understand what I asked her.

"Your baby daddy? Unless you're the virgin Mary."

"Oh, he was here earlier, but he had to work. I wish you could've met him. Maybe next time."

"Oh, if he was here for my bitch, then I'm good. Ok, so can I meet my God baby now?"

"Sure."

We walked together over to the NICU where her baby girl was in the incubator. I washed my hands then the nurse took her out and passed her to me. Lexi was right, she was adorable. As I stared at the precious baby girl, I felt like I'd seen her before in another life. See, I now knew we were going to have a connection.

"Hey little mama, I'm in love already," Lexi whispered in her little ear. I stood there rocking her back and forth. We spent a few more minutes with her before the nurse placed her back into the incubator.

"How long, they keeping her for?" I asked Lexi as we walked back to her room.

"Well, you know she was born premature with jaundice, so she's getting treated for that. So, I guess as soon as that is cleared up and she's at a healthy weight. I go home tomorrow and it is going to be hard for me to leave her up in here."

"Well, she will be in good hands. Plus, you will be up here to make sure of that."

"Yeah, I know."

We got back to the room and talked for a little while longer and then I decided to leave. I was tired as hell.

"A'ight chica, I'm about to go. It was a long day at the shop and these damn feet are killing me. I need to go soak them in some bubble bath."

"Hmm, you were smiling when you said that. Let me find out you got somebody to rub them for you."

"Girl, first you need to feel better. Then I will bring you up to date on my love life."

"Uh huh, my pussy's sore, not my ears, but I hear you," she busted out laughing.

"Get you some rest and call me if you need me."

"A'ight."

I left out and walked to the elevator. I felt my phone vibrating. I reached into my purse and pulled it out. It was Jarvis. "Hey you, I was just gonna call you."

"Is that so? I just realized what time it was. I had not heard from you and I was kind of got worried."

"Oh shit, I meant to call you after I left the shop. Lexi had the baby and I swung by the hospital to check on them."

"Oh ok…You know whenever I don't hear from you, I kind of get worried."

"I know babe, but I'm on my way to the house now. What you got going on tonight?"

"That was what I wanted to find out from you. I mean, we can grab a bite and a movie."

"Sounds like a plan, since this is my last free night. The kids come back tomorrow night."

"Ok, I'll pick you up at ten."

"Ok babe."

I walked to my car and dug into my purse to pull out my key, but quickly realized that it wasn't in there. Damn… I remembered that I had it in my hand when I went to Lexi's room. Fuck, I had to go back up there. I swear, I wanted to cry because my feet were hurting so damn bad. I stood there waiting on the elevator which looked like it was coming from the top floor. I rushed inside and pressed the button for the third floor. A nurse stepped on as I stepped off. We exchanged smiles and I walked to Bianca's room. I was about to knock, but instead I pushed the door and entered.

"I left my key..." I didn't get to finish my sentence because I was shocked as fuck. My husband Mel was sitting in a chair by her bed.

"What the fuck is this?" I managed to ask, while looking at both of their faces.

"Well, look who is here. My wife. Hey honey, how you doing?" That old bitch ass nigga said with a slight grin on his face.

"Bianca, Mel just stopped by to see how me and the baby is doing."

"Really Lexi? So, you are okay with the nigga that put your best friend in the hospital visiting you and shit?"

"Bitch, I ain't did shit to you. Quit lying on me. Matter of fact, do you want to tell this bitch, or should I tell her?"

"Tell me what Lexi? What the fuck is this nigga talking about?" I scooted closer to Lexi's bed.

"Come on y'all. This ain't the motherfucking place for you to bring no drama. My damn baby is in the NICU and y'all supposed to be here supporting me, not up in here settling y'all fucking beefs."

"Nah fuck that. That nigga said y'all got something to tell me. So, speak the fuck up."

"Bitch, ain't nobody scared of yo' police ass. I will body yo' ass if you keep on playing me like I'm a chump." That nigga took a gun out and pointed it at me.

"What you goin' do, shoot me? You a bitch ass nigga that only has balls when you got a weapon in your hand. Shoot then pussy, or bitch up like a hoe."

"Stop, both of you! Just get the fuck out before I call the nurse up in here!" Lexi screamed.

That nigga tucked his gun back in his waist and took a seat, but not before he shot me a devilish grin. I heard the door open and the nurse rushed in.

"Is everything okay? I heard a lot of screaming up in here."

I didn't wait around. I dashed out the room and ran to the elevator. I was pissed the fuck off. That bitch ass nigga just threatened my life and then what the fuck was he saying when he asked if she wanted him to tell me? I knew damn well he wasn't talking about them fucking around. Lexi might've had her fucked up ways, but I knew Mel wasn't her type. Furthermore, we were best friends and she was very loyal. I knew one thing. She had some damn explaining to do as soon as her ass got up out of that hospital.

I got in my car feeling mentally and physically drained. That nigga had got to me. I couldn't believe I had laid down and made babies with his bitch ass. I saw that I would need a restraining order against him ASAP. I pulled out thinking all kind of crazy shit. I swear if, I knew that I could get away with murder, I would definitely kill that nigga my damn self.

That shower was everything that I needed. I got dressed in something comfortable and pinned my weave up. I applied a little make up to hide the bags under my eyes. Lately, I hadn't been able to sleep at night. I just had a lot on my mind. I took one last glance in the mirror, sprayed my body with my favorite perfume and grabbed my Gucci Clutch.

I heard a horn honk and I peeped out of the window. It was Jarvis. I set the alarm, locked the door and stepped out into the chilly night. "Hey babe," I said as he kissed me on the cheek.

"Hey you." I got in the car. He closed my door and got behind the wheel.

"Do you have an idea where you wanna eat?"

"Not really. Shit, we can just grab something at the movies. I'm not fussy tonight at all."

"You sure? I mean, we still have time."

"Yeah, I'm sure babe."

He stopped the car and looked at me. "You a'ight? You seem a little distant?"

I thought about lying to him, but I looked in his eyes and realized he was genuinely concerned. "That nigga pulled a gun on me this evening."

"Say what? He came to the shop? And why the fuck you didn't tell me earlier?"

"This happened at the hospital. When I went to see Lexi, he was there. We got into it and he pulled a fucking gun on me."

"Yo', this shit has got to stop. I been trying to stay out of it, 'cause that is still your husband and children's father, but fuck that. That nigga's going too far now."

He pulled off. I could tell he was upset, because he turned the music up. Kevin Gates's, "Tiger" blasted through the speakers. I wished I hadn't said anything, because I did not want him involved in my drama.

We ended up just grabbing hot dogs from the movie theater. Then we went in to catch the latest Kevin Hart movie that had just hit the theaters. Jarvis was a huge Kevin Hart fan, so even though I wasn't into movies, I decided to support bae. Soon as the movie started, my eyes started feeling heavy and I rested my head on his shoulder. He wrapped his arm around me and seconds later I was out. "Babe wake up." I felt someone shaking me.

"I'm watching the movie," I said as I tried to wake myself up.

"The movie is over boo and you were fast asleep. Let's go."

Damn, I thought as I tried to fully open my eyes.

We walked out and headed towards his car. "I guess your ass was tired. You were out, snoring and all."

"Boy, quit lying. I don't snore." I pushed him playfully.

"Yes, you do." He picked me up and held me up in the air.

"Boy put me down and be careful. Your ass might drop me." I tried to wiggle my way out of his grip. That wasn't happening. He had a strong hold on me as he planted kisses all over my face.

"You know I'm falling for you lady."

"Are you really?" I was curious to hear some more.

"Hell yeah, I'm serious." He kissed my lips and then put my feet back down on the ground. He opened my door and I got in the car. He proceeded to walk around to his side. In a split second, I saw a shadow approach out of nowhere. It looked like there was a man dressed in all black with a mask on and a gun pointed at Jarvis. I couldn't hear what was being said. I lowered my head, trying to find my phone. I saw when the figure raised the gun and fired shots at Jarvis. I heard the operator saying hello on my phone, but I was frozen. I watched as the figure ran in the opposite direction.

"Noooooooooooooooooooooooo!" I screamed from the bottom of my heart.

I opened the car door, ran over to him, lifted his head off the concrete and rested it on my lap. "Hold on baby, hold on. Help! Somebody, please help me. He has been shot. Please somebody!" I yelled out.

An elderly man ran over to me. "Ma'am, I am a certified EMT. Let me check him. Did you call 911?"

"Huh?" I heard him, but it seemed as if he was speaking a different language to me.

"Lady, call 911! This man is bleeding out!" he yelled, snapping me out of my trance.

I ran back to the car and grabbed my cellphone that was still on the seat.

"Hello," I heard the operator say.

"Hello, can you send an ambulance to NCG Cinema on Rockbridge Road."

"What is your name and what is the emergency ma'am?"

"My name is Bianca and my boyfriend has been shot several times."

"Please can you give me the address of where you are?"

"Listen lady. Just send the fucking ambulance."

"Ma'am, where was he shot? Did you see who shot him?"

"He was shot and nah, I ain't see who shot him. Can you just send the damn ambulance already? How the fuck is all these gotdamn questions supposed to help save his life?"

"Calm down ma'am. I'm only trying to do my job. An ambulance is on the way. Please stay on the phone with me until they arrive."

I rushed back over to where the dude was applying pressure to his chest. Tears started rolling down my face as I started whispering pleading prayers. A few seconds later I heard the ambulance, police cars and fire trucks racing through the parking lot.

They rushed over where Jarvis was and demanded that we get out of the way. I watched helplessly as they helped him on the gurney and rushed him into the ambulance. I thought about following the ambulance, but quickly remembered that he drove his car and his keys were in his hand. I looked beside the car and saw them on the ground.

"Ma'am that is evidence. Step away from the car."

"My name is Bianca and I was with Jarvis Coleman."

"We need to ask you some questions about what took place here tonight."

I swear, I wasn't in any condition to answer any more questions. I really needed to be there with Jarvis, letting him know that he wasn't alone. I saw that the detectives were not going to let me leave, so I decided to just let them ask whatever questions they had.

Honestly, I wasn't much help to them, because the shit happened so damn fast. Whoever it was, was wearing a mask and fully dressed in black. After they searched his car and the forensic team scoped out the scene, collecting the shells that were left on the ground, a detective gave me the keys and told me I could go.

I wasted no time as I jumped in the car and pulled off. I learned from the officer that they took him to Grady Memorial Hospital, which was one of the best hospitals in the Atlanta area for trauma.

Speeding down the street, my heart was heavy as hell as I prayed for him to pull through. I knew it was pretty bad. Although I wasn't really religious, I still believed that God worked miracles and he could make the possible out of the impossible. I wiped the tears from my face as I tried to stay focused on the road.

I pulled into the hospital parking lot, parked, rushed out of the car and ran into the hospital. "Hello ma'am, I am here to check the status of Jarvis Coleman."

"Hold on. He just got here. He is in surgery."

I let out a long sigh. That meant my baby was still breathing. "Thank you. Please let me know if anything changes."

"Are you a relative? Because you know he is a victim of a shooting and we don't give out information if he you are not a member of his family."

"Yes, I'm his fiancée. I was with him when he got shot."

"Ok, I apologize. I will keep you posted of any changes." Her tone changed to sympathetic.

I walked away to sit in a corner away from everybody. I needed a second to gather my thoughts. My mind was racing as I tried to figure out who could have done that to him. One of the detectives asked me if I thought he was robbed, but it wasn't a robbery. He always wore a chain and expensive bracelet worth thousands of dollars, but whoever shot him did not take them. He had money and credit cards, but none of that was touched. So, to be honest, it wasn't a robbery. Whoever it was had come directly for him, but why though? He wasn't in the streets. He had a legit business and worked hard every day. When he wasn't at work, we were together.

My head was spinning and I had one of the worst migraines. I realized that I didn't know a lot about him. I didn't even know who his family was. I felt helpless that I could not call anyone for him. I just sat there waiting. Every time someone came out, I popped my head up, bracing myself for the worst, but expecting the best. God knows, it had been the happiest time of my life and there was no way I thought he was going to be taken away from me that fast.

I deserved some happiness and Jarvis has been giving me that. I just knew I couldn't lose it, so I leaned against the wall and just closed my eyes. I was hoping it was just a nightmare and I would be waking up real soon. I heard my phone vibrating. I reached for it, although I wasn't in the mood to talk to anyone. It could've been the kids. My aunts would be flying in with them tomorrow.

I looked at the caller ID and noticed that it was Lexi. As much as I wanted to answer and cry my heart out to my friend, I couldn't forget the incident that had happened earlier. She had some fucking explaining to do. I put my phone on silent and threw it back in my bag. Memories of the situation from earlier started invading my mental space. My mind flashed back to Mel pulling that gun out on me. That was when I started thinking that Mel could be the one who shot Jarvis? Nah, I tried to dismiss that thought out of my head, but it lingered around.

CHAPTER TEN

Lexi

"I can't fucking believe you took it there with Bianca? Why the fuck would you do that?"

"Man, why the fuck not? That bitch came up in here popping shit. I ain't no chump and I'm tired of that bitch acting like she can keep carrying a nigga. I swear, I will body that bitch for real."

"I don't give a fuck about what y'all got going on. Just don't fucking drag me in y'all shit. I want to tell her about us on my own time, not when you mad and want to throw me in the middle. That's all I'm saying. Your baby is next door sick. Shit, be a little bit considerate."

"I feel you on that, but shit. You checking the wrong motherfucking person, for real. You should've checked that bitch when she was up in here disrespecting me. I guess I see where your loyalty really is. Maybe y'all two bitches should get together."

"Are you fucking serious? You're being disrespectful right now. All I was saying is, you know me and her are friends. Why throw that shit out there like that?"

"Fuck all that friend shit. Let's keep it one hunnit. Y'all friendship been over since the day you got on your knees and sucked my dick. So, you can stop fucking pretending and acting like you scared of that bitch."

Those words stung my fucking soul. I looked at him as he spat venom at me. I was the woman who had just given birth to his child a few hours ago. "You know what Mel, I ain't even gonna go there wit' yo ass."

"Mane, fuck all that shit you talking 'bout. I'm about to bounce. Call me when you ready to leave tomorrow."

"You leaving? You didn't even see your child. What kind of shit you on nigga?"

"Lexi, I'm pissed the fuck off. I will see the baby tomorrow. I'm out." Before I could respond, that nigga walked off and out the door.

Fuck my life, I thought. See, there I was thinking that having that nigga's baby would kind of make him change his ways a little. Now, I knew that was not working. His ass had got me in some shit with Bianca and I could tell that her ass was angry as fuck. Knowing her, she wasn't going to let it go. I needed to hurry up and get my strength back just in case that bitch tried to start some shit. I needed to figure out a way to approach the fucking situation.

I was excited to be getting up out of the hospital the next day. The food was horrible, plus I needed to go and prepare for my baby coming home. I thought, I had two more months to get everything ready for her, but I was wrong. I needed to set her crib up and wash all her clothing. One thing I could say about her daddy was, he made sure she had everything. I just hoped he planned to be there hands on.

I sat with my baby for a while, just talking and singing sweet lullabies to her. Each day that I spent with her, I realized that how much more I'd fallen in love with her. If I'd never done anything great in my life, I could say I outdid myself with my baby girl. All we needed was for daddy to marry mommy and our life would be so complete.

I took a shower after I got back to the room. It was my last night there and I was too excited. I turned the TV on and saw breaking news flash across the screen. There was a shooting at a movie theater in Stone Mountain. According to the reporter, it was a black male. That was when it hit me that had not heard from Mel since he left.

I grabbed my cellphone and dialed his number. The phone kept ringing the first few times and then the fourth time, it went straight to voicemail. I thought it was because he was trying to call me when I was calling him. I waited a few minutes, but my phone didn't ring. I dialed his number again and it went straight to voicemail. That nigga had turned his phone off. I tried calling his work phone and it just rang. I could see that he was playing games. I swear, I wished I could fucking leave up out of there right then. A tear fell from my eye, as anger invaded my heart. I was in a hospital room alone, while that nigga was running the motherfucking streets with those old, stinking ass bitches. "Nooooo!" I threw my phone across the room, not giving a fuck if it broke, or not. I was hurting and that was all that really mattered at the time.

I had no one to talk to. I got up from the bed, grabbed my phone and dialed Bianca's number. Her phone just rang. Damn, where the fuck was that bitch at? Shit, they were probably still creeping, but pretended to hate each other in my face. All sorts of crazy, irrational thoughts ran through my head.

It was a little after nine am and that nigga still wasn't there to pick me up. I had dialed his number over thirty times and the phone kept going to voicemail. Ughh, I hated that shit. I remembered one of my clients telling me about LYFT, which was a taxi service that would pick me up and drop me off. I Googled it and within minutes I was set up and ready to go. I requested their service and grabbed my stuff. My heart was breaking, because I had to leave my baby behind, but the doctor assured me that her treatment was going along well and she would be home in a no time. The APP on the phone let me know that my ride was there. The nurse pushed the wheelchair out in the front. I thanked her and got in car.

We pulled up to the house and I jumped out, forgetting to thank the elderly woman for the ride. I was even angrier when I noticed Mel's Range Rover parked in the driveway. I searched for my keys and wasted no time opening that damn door. That nigga was going to catch it when I got my hands on his ass. I ran up the stairs and pushed my room door open. I saw that nigga knocked out under the cover. I pulled the cover back and that was when I got the motherfucking shock of my life.

"Yo' nigga wake your bitch ass up! What the fuck are you doing in my bed with a bitch?"

"What the fuck you doing here?" He sat up, grabbed his boxers and hurriedly put them on.

"What the fuck am I doing here? Did you forget that this is my motherfucking house?"

"Baby, who is this and what is she talking about?" That high yellow bitch, who looked like her pussy stink said.

"Bitch, I'm Lexi and this is my motherfucking house. You are in my bed bitch and this my nigga that you just fucked. Anything else you want to know?"

"Mel, is that true? You told me you were separated from your wife."

That nigga looked very aggravated and it seemed like he wished he could just disappear.

"Man, y'all need to chill. I mean, c'mon. It ain't no need for all this drama shit."

"Boy, fuck you. Get your shit and your bitch and get out of my shit."

"I ain't goin' be too many more bitches. I know you upset and shit, but you need to check your nigga, 'cause we've been fucking around for over a year and not once did he mention a bitch outside of his wife. Listening to you talk, I doubt you the bitch that he's married to."

I lunged toward that bitch, but didn't have a chance to touch her, because he jumped between us. Pushing his fucking hand away, I said, "Don't fucking touch me nigga. You left me and your child up in the hospital to be up in my house with your whore. This is how you do me?" The tears forced their way out onto my face.

"Man, my bad yo'. I didn't mean for you to see none of this. I just slept too late yo'."

"Babe, you apologizing to this bitch? Because, I mean fuck her."

"Shut up bitch! Matter of fact, put your clothes on and bounce!" he yelled.

"You know what nigga. You can put on a front right now, but yo' black ass will be right back, sucking on my pussy and begging me to be with you." She jumped off the bed and grabbed her clothes.

Hate filled my heart for that nigga and that bitch!

"No, you need to go with her ass, 'cause you ain't staying up in here."

"Lexi, chill the fuck out B. You just need time to calm down."

"Nigga, fuck you. I should've left yo' ass in jail, but guess what? I am done playing the motherfucking fool. Find you another dumb bitch."

"Man, stop tryna carry me like I'm a chump. A nigga don't have to be up in here. I'm here 'cause I fucks wit' you shawty. Don't ever think a nigga need you." He grabbed his clothes and walked off down the stairs. The bitch must've sensed danger, because her ass ran right behind him, cussing. I dragged everything off my bed and threw it down the stairs.

"Fuck you Melvinnnnnnnnnnnnn!" I screamed out. I took a seat on the floor and it was then that all the tears poured out. I was hurting so bad, my chest started to hurt. "How could you do this to me Mel? I risked everything for you," I cried.

There was no way I could get past that. He had messed everything up, by disrespecting me in the worse way. How could he bring his whore in the bed we shared? Oh, my God, was that my karma for taking him away from Bianca? It hurt so damn bad. I tried my best to catch my breath, but it felt like I couldn't breathe.

CHAPTER ELEVEN

Bianca

It had been five days since Jarvis got shot. Thank God, he made it through after going through two surgeries. The doctors did say the next seventy-two hours would be critical. I swear, my ass had never prayed so much in a lifetime the way I prayed every day since he got shot. I got on my knees like my momma taught me when I was younger and I poured my soul out.

I was so caught up in my thoughts that I didn't notice that we were no longer alone. "Hello. How are you?"

I hesitated, but then answered. "I'm good. Who are you?"

"I'm Dorothy, Jarvis's mother and this is his little sister. We got word that my baby almost died and I was sick myself, so I had to get clearance from my doctor to travel."

"You must be his lady friend? He called home several times just going on and on about you. He couldn't wait to bring you and the kids home for the holidays."

I smiled, because of what she had said. I saw that I was no secret and he was serious about us. I stayed there a little longer and then decided to leave. His mom was there with him, so I knew he was not alone anymore. He was in a medical induced coma for a few days and I couldn't wait until he could talk to me. I missed our daily laughs at nothing in particular. We always found a way to keep each other smiling. Tears welled up in my eyes as I remembered the happy times.

"I love you, bae, but I got to go home. I'll be back tomorrow to see you." I squeezed his hand and kissed him on the forehead.

"It was nice meeting you Miss Dorothy."

"Come here child. Give me a hug. My son accepts you, so I have no choice but to accept you. I only hope you can help him get out of those streets. I lost his daddy just like this and he's my only boy. God knows my heart can't take no more loss. I been begging him for years to get out of those streets because the truth is, those streets don't love nobody. He tried to convince me that he was no longer in the streets, because he got his own business. Well, I might be old, but I ain't no fool. I just hope you can talk him out of it." She took my hand and placed in hers.

"Help me save my baby from those streets."

I smiled at her and nodded. "I'll see you later." I removed my hand and walked out of the room. I hurried to the elevator, because I needed to get out of that hospital. I felt like I couldn't breathe. I needed air, fast.

I opened my car door and stumbled in. It took a few seconds for me to catch my breath and digest what that woman had said to me. Jarvis was in the streets? Was she mistaken? He had his own legit business. As a matter of fact, that was how I met him. I was confused. His mother seemed sure about what she was saying to me. She even went as far as saying that was how his father was killed. I remembered him telling me that his father was killed violently, but he didn't go into the specifics. I didn't push him, because I didn't want him to feel like I was intruding. I just figured it was painful for him, and he wasn't ready to talk about it. None of it made sense to me. Was his mother right? If he was in the streets could that be the reason he was in the hospital fighting for his life? I rested my head on the steering wheel. If that was true, why would he lie like that? Why would he pretend like he owned a business? I shook my head in disbelief and pulled off.

***

I took a hot bath and tried to get some sleep, but honestly, I had too much on my mind. What Jarvis's mother said to me kept playing over and over in my mind. Also, the shit with Lexi and Mel was also on my mind. I hadn't had the time to address the shit with her, because she was on maternity leave and I'd been working at the shop and going to the hospital every day. I knew that I needed some fucking answers fast. That was all I could think about before I dozed off.

After Jarvis got shot, I asked my aunt if she could keep the kids for a few more days. She agreed and they were flying back in the morning. I wasn't going to lie, I was ready to see my babies for real, because in the midst of the storm, they were my calm. They were the ones who kept me going. I got dressed and raced to the airport. I knew their plane landed at nine am and it was a few minutes after nine. There was no way I wanted to leave my babies waiting.

I parked and walked over to the Delta Terminal. I waited for about ten minutes, and then I spotted them walking up. My heart started racing fast as I rushed towards them.

"Hey my loves," I said to them both as I grabbed them. "Hey ma," they said in unison.

"Hey auntie," I turned to my mother's younger sister and hugged her.

"Let's get y'all bags, so we can go."

After we grabbed the bags, we walked to the car. "How was y'all trip?"

"It was fun ma. We went to Disney World and the beach almost every day," Trisha said.

"Aww, sound like y'all had fun. I'm jealous," I joked.

"Child, they had a great time. I swear, if I didn't know better, I would think they didn't want to come back home."

"I can only imagine. I am happy they had a great time."

We got in the car and I pulled off. They were chatting, but my mind was racing, trying to figure out how I was going to tell them that their daddy did not live there anymore. I realized there was no good way to say it, but it had to be said. To be honest, I was worried about how it was going to hurt them, but I was there for them and I knew we would get through it.

I pulled into the driveway and they got out. "I know y'all gonna grab y'all bags," I said as I walked off to open the door. I quickly disarmed the alarm.

"Come on auntie."

We walked into the house and I locked the door. I was still being careful just in case Mel decided to show his face around there. The kids dropped their luggage in the den and then raced upstairs to their bedrooms. I guess they were excited to be home.

"Come on auntie. Let me show you your room." We walked upstairs and I showed her the guest room.

"These sheets are clean. You have towels in the top drawer and your bathroom is to the left. Make yourself comfortable."

I then went downstairs to grab the kids' luggage out of the den. Their asses know better than that, but since they were just getting back and I missed them, I would let it fly. "Mommy, where is daddy at? I thought he was home." Melvin Junior said.

I was so not ready, but I had to make myself ready. "Go get your sister. I need to talk to y'all."

He ran up the stairs and I took e few seconds to gather my thoughts. I knew it was a delicate situation that I needed to enter with caution. "Ma, where you at?" Melvin Jr. yelled out.

"I'm in the den," I hollered back.

They walked in. "Sit down, I need to talk to y'all."

They sat down, looking at me like they were ready to hear what I had to say. "Listen y'all. I need to tell you something very important." I inhaled, exhaled and

140

braced myself. "Your daddy and I are separated and he won't be coming back home," I blurted out.

"Where is daddy ma? What you mean, he ain't coming back?" Melvin Jr. asked.

"He no longer lives here, but y'all will still see him. Nobody can take that away."

"So, you and daddy don't love each other no more?" Melvin Jr. asked.

"Listen baby, sometimes people outgrow one another. That doesn't mean we hate each other. Listen daddy and I still love y'all and that's all that really matters."

"Okay, can we go now?" he asked.

"Sure."

I was shocked. They handled it better than I thought they would. Shit, I was nervous for nothing. Ok, now that, that was out of the way, I could refocus on Jarvis. I was happy that my aunt agreed to spend a few weeks with us, so she could help me with the kids. I was mentally drained, for real.

CHAPTER TWELVE

Lexi

I was happy as hell, because I was on my way to pick up my baby girl. She was finally released from the hospital. I sure wished her daddy was there with me, but I was still pissed off at him. I had to go out and buy a whole damn mattress, because of his old trifling ass bringing that hoe up in my house. Just thinking about it made me upset all over again. His ass had been blowing up my phone, begging me to talk to him. My heart wanted to take him back because I loved him, but I was still angry. There was no way I was going to let him back in so damn easily. I pulled into the hospital parking lot, parked, and grabbed my baby's diaper bag and her car seat.

***

Soon as we got home and I got my baby settled, I heard my front door open. I panicked, because I thought it was an intruder. I jumped up off the coach and that was when I realized it was Mel. All along that nigga had my house key and I had totally forgot. "What are you doing here?"

"Man, chill out Lexi. I come to see my daughter."

"You can't just run up in here. This is my shit and I told you I don't want you here anymore."

"Man, chill out wit' all that. You my bitch and that's my pussy. I ain't tryna hear all that shit you tryna spit. Where my baby at?"

"She's upstairs," I said reluctantly.

That old ignorant ass nigga walked off on me and up the stairs. I swear, I missed his ass, but I wouldn't dare let him know that. I waited a few minutes then I tiptoed up the stairs. The door was cracked opened, so I peeped in on them. It warmed my heart to see him sitting in the chair rocking her and holding her on his chest. The nigga that acted all tough and shit was looking real emotional. I eased away from the door and walked back down the stairs.

About an hour later he came down the stairs.

"Yo', she's beautiful just like her mama. Come here man."

He wrapped his arms around me. "Listen man, a nigga's sorry for that shit. I was just going through shit in the streets and you wasn't here. I ain't making no excuse, 'cause I'm a man and I'm gonna own up to my shit. All I can ask you for is a chance to make it up to you."

My eyes were already filled with tears. I loved that man and I just hoped he would get his shit together, because I couldn't live like that.

We stood in the middle of the living room hugging when I heard the doorbell ring. *Man, who the fuck is that ringing off my doorbell*, I thought.

"Who the fuck is that?" Mel asked.

"Man, I have no fucking idea. Maybe somebody selling some shit."

DEVOTED TO A STREET KING

He let me go and I walked off to check through the peep hole. My body froze as I took a second glance.

CHAPTER THIRTEEN

Bianca

Nia, one of our mutual friends, told me that Lexi had brought the baby home from the hospital. I was still angry with her, but that was my God daughter and I had a lot of baby stuff that I bought. I wasn't going to be petty and not give it to her. I thought about calling Lexi, but quickly decided not to. She would probably just ignore my calls especially if she thought it has something to do with the conversation we had at the hospital.

I pulled up at her house and quickly spotted a Range Rover that resembled Mel's. I jumped out of my car, leaving all that shit behind. I ran around the back of the vehicle to check the license plate and sure enough, it was Melvin's Range Rover.

I anxiously rang the doorbell. I knew those motherfuckers had some explaining to do. I waited a few seconds and then pressed down harder on it. I heard when the lock clicked and the door opened.

"Hey girl, what you doing here?"

I didn't say a word. I just pushed the door wide open and dashed past her.

"What are you doing Bianca? You just busting up in my shit? I mean, I know you eager to see the baby, but she's sleeping."

"Bitch, you know damn well, I ain't looking for no damn baby! Cut the fucking games out. Where the fuck is my husband?"

"Your husband? Why would your husband be up in my shit? I just got home."

"That's Melvin's truck parked outside of your house. So, unless you're the one driving it, which I doubt, where the fuck he at?"

"Bianca, you're tripping. Melvin is not here and you are just paranoid because of that dumb shit he said the other day. That boy was only trying to ruffle your feathers. I see that he did just that, because look at you, behaving like a crazy woman."

"Bitch, fuck you. Keep that motherfucking speech, for real. See, I don't know what's going on, but best believe when I do find out, I'm going to beat your motherfucking ass. Don't get it fucked up. I ain't goin' to beat your ass over that bitch ass nigga. I'ma beat your ass because you were supposed to be my bitch and you entertaining that nigga. What kind of shit you on?"

"Like I said, you tripping and I ain't met a bitch yet that can whoop my ass outside of my dead mama. So, keep your fucking threats over there. I understand that nigga's fucking around on you, but you barking up the wrong tree. You need to be fucking looking at all those other bitches he running around town with. Matter of fact, I heard he had a motherfucking baby mama."

"Bitch, who is your baby daddy? As close as we are, why I ain't never met that invisible ass nigga? Even when we had your baby shower at the shop, why he ain't show his motherfucking face? Bitch, you just popped out of the blue with a stomach… hmm you're real suspicious."

"Haha. You know what. Get out of my house. Who I'm fucking, or not fucking should be the least of your worries, especially since your husband's slinging dick all over town."

"All you need to do is make sure he ain't slinging no dick your way, 'cause if I ever find out I'ma drag your ass," I said and stormed out of the house.

I dashed down the driveway and popped my trunk. I grabbed a large wrench and busted all of Mel's windows out of his Range. Glass shattered everywhere, but I didn't give a fuck. I then got in my car, reversed and left. I did see a figure in the window right before I pulled off.

I was so fucking heated. I knew that Melvin's coward ass was in that house and that old lying ass bitch was covering for him. Oh, my God, how could that bitch do that to me? I trusted her. I told that bitch everything that we were going through. My head was spinning as I tried my best to control my car. My vision was getting blurry, so I decided to pull over, so I could get myself together. "Damn you Melvin! I fucking hate you!" I yelled out and started beating my steering wheel. Could it be possible that the entire time that he was cheating, he was cheating with my best friend?

After a few minutes of crying and trying to make some sense out of what was going on, I wiped my face with a napkin and then pulled off. I needed to get home to my children.

***

I walked in the house, threw my bag on the kitchen table and grabbed me a glass. I needed a damn drink, so I grabbed a bottle of Gin and poured it. I needed something strong to help me get through the pain that I was feeling. I put two cubes of ice in the glass and took two bug gulps. I rested against the counter for support. Tears rolled down my face as I felt the lowest form of betrayal by someone that I loved and respected. A nigga was going to be a dog, but us bitches were supposed to stick together. It hurt even more, because that bitch didn't have the guts to tell me what was really going on. I mean, if you were woman enough to fuck my nigga, at least put your big girl drawers on and admit that shit.

"Baby, you alright?" My auntie placed her hand on my shoulder.

"Auntie, I am just dealing with a lot right now."

"I don't mean to pry, but I can't help but notice that Melvin is not here. Is everything okay in your marriage?"

"We are getting a divorce auntie. I've been dealing with him and his cheating ways for years. I just got tired of it. I didn't tell the family, but a few months ago, he beat on me, and I ended up in the hospital. Auntie, I couldn't take anymore."

"Put his hands on you? That son of a bitch done lost his rabbit ass mind. You need to get a gun and shoot his ass if he comes near you again. Baby girl, you deserve so much better, I always thought you was too good of a woman for his old, black, ugly ass."

"I am just done. He got locked up after he came up in here not too long ago. I just don't want him showing up now that the kids are back."

"You need to take your behind down to the courthouse and get a restraining order against him. Don't hesitate to divorce his ass."

"That's what I plan on doing."

"Pour me one of those. That nigga just pissed me off. I will kill him my damn self. Is this house in your name, or both?"

"Both, but I don't give a damn. I will walk away from all this shit."

"Foolishness! You busted yo' ass in this marriage and you have his kids. Get yourself a good lawyer and tell them about his infidelity and how he beat on you. Trust me, the judge will have mercy on you. Those judges don't like no woman beater. You deserve this and so much more for putting up with his ass for all these years."

I took a few more sips of my drink as I thought about what she was saying. I could tell my auntie was hell back in her younger days. She was nothing to be played with.

We sat in the kitchen talking about life in general. I did go ahead and tell her about Jarvis. She was happy to know that I was somewhat happy. However, she did warn me not to move too fast, because these niggas were not worth shit.

"Well, I need to run by the hospital. You can order pizza and wings for you and the kids, 'cause more than likely, I won't be back in time for dinner."

"Nonsense! I'm about to thaw out some chicken, so I can make some chicken and broccoli. You know damn well I don't like all that fast food."

I smiled at her, because I sure knew better. Her ass had no problem cooking every damn day.

"Alright, well, call me if you need me. I'm about to take a shower so I can go."

"Baby girl, please be careful out there. That nigga is angry and bitter. You have no idea what he's capable of doing. Watch your surroundings at all times."

"Thanks auntie. I got it."

I smiled and walked out the kitchen. I did make a mental note of what she had said to me. I knew Mel ass was involved in the streets and he was always talking about what he did to niggas who disrespected him. I didn't put anything past him for real.

***

I walked into the hospital room to see that my boo was awake. Shit, why didn't I get a phone call about that? Nonetheless, I was so damn happy. His mama and sister were present and boy were they chatting it up. They were so caught up in their conversation that they didn't see me when I entered the room. I cleared my throat to make my presence known. "Oh, hey there dear," his mama greeted me.

"Hey. Oh, look who is alive and kicking. Hey you," I walked over and gave him a long, drawn out hug. My heart was jumping with joy.

"I miss you babe, but mama told me you ain't left my side."

"Uh huh, you know damn well I wasn't going nowhere." I sat on the edge of the bed, rubbing his leg through the blanket.

"So, what is the doctor saying?"

"He said everything looks good. I'll be in here maybe another week or so."

"That's good. Did the police come talk to you?"

"Yeah, they came up here, but I ain't had shit to tell them." His tone was a little harsh and his face expression changed.

I could see that he was uneasy, so I dropped the subject. "I'm just happy that we didn't lose you."

"Ma, you know a nigga ain't going nowhere." He reached up and grabbed my hand.

"Well, now that you're here, we're going to run to the hotel to shower and then grab a bite. A'ght baby, I will talk to you later. Love you." His mother leaned over and kissed him.

"A'ight bro. Love you," his sister said.

"See y'all later," I said before they left the room.

"Now, it's just me and my lady. Come over here and give you daddy a proper hello."

"Boy stop, with yo' nasty self." I laid my head on his chest.

"How you holding up babe?"

"I'm good. Just been worried about you."

"I know, but guess what? Your nigga is here and I ain't going nowhere anytime soon."

Soon as he said that, I recalled everything his mother said to me about him being involved in the streets. I thought about confronting him, but quickly dismissed that idea. I wasn't a cold bitch, so it could wait until he got home.

We hung out for a little while longer. I helped the nurse with him before I left. That night was different when I left the hospital. My heart was happier and I wasn't crying and feeling broken. Instead, my heart was in a better place, because he was awake. Although he wasn't in the best of shape, I was convinced he would be better soon.

I saw a shadow on my left. I quickly turned, but nothing was there. I stopped for a few seconds, but didn't see, or hear anything other than cars passing by. I started walking to my car. When I got in, I quickly locked the doors. I knew there was somebody following me when I walked out of the hospital. I reached into my glove compartment and took out my gun. I placed it on the seat next to me and pulled off, still looking around nervously.

When I got on my street, I kept looking in my mirrors to see if anyone was following me. I didn't see anyone. I pulled into the garage and held my gun in my hand when I got out of the car. It may seem like I was paranoid, but I wasn't.

CHAPTER FOURTEEN

Lexi

Bitches were sleeping on me, because I sat around laughed with them. They thought it was cool to talk to me like they were crazy. See, that was the thing. Mel was Bianca's husband and she had all rights to him, so I kept my mouth closed. But see, she and Mel were over, and since I was the one who went and got the nigga out of jail, technically, he was mine.

That bitch called herself threatening me. Bianca knew damn well that I was nice with these hands, so she was only yapping off at the mouth. I knew it wasn't over between us, but best believe I was ready to fight for what was rightfully mine.

My phone started ringing. I looked at the caller ID and it was my big mouthed ass sister. Her ass had been on vacation and was just returning. "Hello, look who finally found time to check on her big sister and niece," I said sarcastically.

"Bitch, open the damn door. I got to pee." She stood there doing the pee dance.

I got up and walked to the door. I should've left her ass out there so she could piss on herself, but I unlocked the door.

She ran inside, threw her bag on the floor and ran upstairs to the bathroom.

"Damn bitch, why you ain't use the bathroom where you were?" I asked as I locked the door.

Her ass was in there messing around with my baby, because I heard her talking and shit. "If you wake her up, you goin' sit there and rock her back to sleep!" I yelled up the stairs.

"She was awake." She walked down the stairs with the baby in her arms. "Sis, she is beautiful. Of course, she looks like her auntie. Ain't that right Pookie?"

"Bitch, don't start with that Pookie shit. Her name is Diamond."

"Bitch, where her daddy at?"

"Somewhere in them damn streets."

"Has her step mama seen her yet?"

"Fuck you hoe. My baby ain't got no damn step mama, but if you talking about Mel's wife, yeah. She came to the hospital talking 'bout she wants to see her God baby. Then bitch, she left and forgot her keys. When she came back, Mel was sitting by the bed. Girl, the bitch went off."

"Bitch, you're lyin'. You a good one, 'cause I would've been told that bitch I was fucking her nigga. I mean, fucking with me that business would've been mine and all. The only thing that bitch would've been able to keep would be her damn kids."

"Girl, ain't nobody tripping off Bianca. I should've stopped talking to that bitch a long time ago. Her ass acts like her shit don't stink. Then she had the nerve to pop up, talking about if she finds out that Mel and I are fucking around, she goin' drag me."

My sister stood up. "That hoe said what? Bitch, I know one thing, you might not want to whoop that bitch's ass, but I have no problem doing it. I live for that shit. That bitch better run along and find somebody else to play with."

"Girl, I laughed at that silly bitch. I told Mel, he better get his baby mama before I make an example out of her."

"What did he say?"

"Girl he snapped on her at the hospital and even pulled a gun on her."

"That nigga is a fool. I told you he ain't wrapped too tight."

"Enough about them. How was your trip with yo' boo?"

"Child, we had a blast. Jamaica was so damn fun, especially Dunns River Falls.

"Well, I'm happy that you had a great time. You deserve to be happy."

"Girl, yes. I hate that he had to go back to work as soon as we got back. We need to plan a dinner, or something real soon."

"That'll work."

We ended up chilling for a little while longer before she left. I stayed up chilling with my baby and wondering where her daddy was. I hadn't heard from him all day, but I knew he was out grinding, so I didn't bother him. I picked up the phone and dialed his number, but got no answer. I threw the phone on the sofa and got up to make my baby a bottle, trying not to get into my feelings too much.

***

CHAPTER FIFTEEN

THREE WEEKS LATER...

Bianca

"You good?" I asked Jarvis.

He was finally released from the hospital and I was driving him home. It was amazing how well he was doing. He was up and about. He said he still was in pain, but other than that, he was good. On the other hand, I was kind of worried, because whoever shot him was still out here. I hadn't asked him anything about it since that day he caught an attitude. I was going to give him a few days, because that was a conversation that we needed to have.

He gave me the address and I pulled into the driveway. I was shocked. That nigga lived in nothing short of a mansion. I had to press a code to get through the gate. It was a brick, two story house that resembled one that a celebrity would live in. I hid my surprise and grabbed his bags out of the car while he got out and walked up to the door.

He walked in and I followed him. As if the outside wasn't beautiful enough, the inside was breathtaking, from the plush carpet, to the marble floors. The chandelier that was hanging in the hallway looked like it was made from pure crystals. The living room furniture was expensive and smelled like fresh leather. Who the fuck was that nigga? I knew damn well he didn't pay for all that shit off a locksmith business income.

"Make yourself comfortable babe."

"Sure."

His phone started ringing. "Excuse me babe." He walked off before he answered it.

Hmmm, that was strange, he never left to answer his phone. I wasn't feeling that shit and I needed to address it shit sooner rather than later. Soon as he walked back into the room, I looked at him. "Listen babe, I was going to wait until you feel better, but we need to talk. Sit down."

"Damn bae, you a'ight?" He looked at me suspiciously.

"Yeah, I'm good. We've been dealing with each other for a while now and I thought we had a certain level of respect for each other. I share things with you that I haven't shared with others. I really thought we were straight up with each other, but I think you were not."

He stood up and looked at me with a grin on his face. "Man, get to the point. What the fuck you tryna say?"

"Don't talk to me like you done lost your damn mind. I know you got shot, but that ain't got shit to do with yo' brain."

"Man, my bad. I'm a straightforward nigga. I can't take that beating around the bush shit. Just spit it out Bianca."

"What do you really do for a living?"

He chuckled. "Bianca, you know what I do for a living. Ain't that how we met baby?"

"Jarvis, quit playing with me. I know for a fucking fact that business is only a cover up for whatever the fuck you into."

"Man, what the fuck you saying? I have no idea where you getting your info from, but I say they feeding you bullshit. You goin' believe what other motherfuckers say and not what your nigga's saying? That's some bullshit."

"Listen, your mama begged me to help get you out the streets. She had no idea that I didn't know what you really do for a living. I was shocked as hell and now that I see where you live, this ain't come from no damn locksmith company. So, before I walk out of this fucking house and your life, you better start talking nigga."

He looked at me like I was a beast with two heads. "Man, sit down. I knew this shit was coming. I wish people would just stay the hell out of my business."

I gritted on that nigga. I wasn't trying to hear the shit he was talking about. All I wanted to know was, what the fuck was he involved in.

"Bianca baby listen. I'ma keep it one hunnit with you. I can't tell you too much, because the less you know, the better it is for you. Just in case anything is to pop off, I don't want to put you in a fucked-up position. Listen, you're right. My locksmith company is just a front, so I can clean my money. I am a street king, meaning I move major dope and guns through these streets. You know how we met and when I started falling for you, I didn't know how to tell you what I really do out here. I got workers who run my shit, so I don't really get my hands dirty."

Slap! Slap! My hand caught his left cheek twice.

"Nigga you got up every day pretending like you're are at work and shit and all along you doing some illegal shit. Why couldn't you trust me enough to tell me? Do you know how betrayed I felt when your mama was begging me to help get her baby out of the streets? That was some shit that I knew nothing about. So, you know who shot you? Is that why you got so mad when I mentioned the police?"

"Man, you ain't goin' understand, but I ain't no nickle and dime nigga. On any given day, I move keys of cocaine. This is major, so with that comes the hate from those niggas. I try to keep you out of that part of my life. I don't want a nigga to feel like they get to me by touching you. Can you understand that shawty? I would lose my fucking mind if anything was to happen to you. I love you Bianca. I want to make you my wife..."

Did I hear that nigga, right? There that nigga was, telling me he was a drug kingpin and yet talking about he wanted to get married. I was no stranger to that lifestyle, because Mel was a lower level drug dealer, but I had never messed with a kingpin. I knew for a fact that they were the ones the Feds went after. Matter of fact, the nigga almost lost his life behind that.

"Listen up, I just got away from another drug dealer and I don't plan on being with another one. I'm not going to spend the rest of my life worrying about you late nights, or living in no visitation rooms. I ain't built for that shit."

"Bianca, boo, I've been in this business for over ten years and I've managed to stay off the police's radar 'cause I ain't one of those other niggas out there. I'm a businessman, so I strategize my every move. I have a few businesses that I'm using to clean up my money. Shawty, this ain't my life. I plan on getting out of it one day."

"I hear you… I just don't know if this is for me right now. I got my kids to worry about. I don't want to bring any danger their way. You know?"

"Bianca, quit making up all those fucking excuses. We been together for months and not one time did I bring any kind of drama your way. I made sure you were not involved in anything, so for you to come at me now, 'cause you done discovered some shit is straight bullshit. Shawty, I'm a real street nigga and I know to handle mine. Believe me, niggas caught me off guard, 'cause I was out with you and I let my guard down a little, but trust me, niggas gon' pay."

"I'm getting ready to go home. I got a lot of shit on my mind and just need some time to think for real."

"A'ight that's cool, but don't let nothing let you lose out on a good nigga. It's me and you babe."

I didn't respond. I just grabbed my purse and let myself out. He stood in the doorway watching me. I backed out and then pulled off. My heart was pulled in all different positions. I loved that man and the way he treated me, but I couldn't help but think about the lies he'd told me numerous times. Why did he think it was ok to lie to me? God, all I wanted was a nigga who didn't lie, or play games with me.

I stopped by the shop. Nia was supposed to be there by herself, so I swung through to make sure everything was running smoothly. The closer I got to the shop, the more I felt uneasy, but I figured it was because I did not eat all day. I had to do better when it came down to taking care of myself. I parked, turned the car off, grabbed my purse and got out. I walked up to the door, opened it and stopped dead in my tracks. My entire shop was fucked up. All my supplies were all over the floor. There were broken bottles and paint on the floor and walls. The further I walked, the more my heart sank. Who the fuck would do that to me? I grabbed my phone and dialed 911. After I spoke to them, I dialed Nia's number. She was supposed to open the shop, but she wasn't there. Tears rolled down my face as I saw everything that I worked for damaged. All the mirrors were broken up, the bathroom was flooded and graffiti was all over my walls. The worst of it all was some sticky looking thing that resembled shit. I wanted to throw up instantly.

I ran out of the shop and got in my car. I tried to catch my breath. I was hurt, but I was angry as fuck. I spent all my life earning money to make my salon one of the best in this city and some hateful ass bitch, or nigga walked up in there and fucked all my shit up in the blink of an eye. I dried the tears that were rolling down my face. I heard my phone ringing. I looked and saw that it was Jarvis calling. I pressed ignore. I would call him back when I finished talking to the police, who were pulling into the parking lot. I got out the car and waited for them to get out and approach me.

"You called the police about vandalism to your business?"

"Yes, I did. Come with me."

I walked off and the two officers followed close behind.

"Ma'am, first I need your name. Then tell us what happened and what time you got here."

I went on to tell them what they wanted to know. They then walked around examining and taking pictures, while writing in their little notebooks.

"Ma'am, I need the names and contact information for everyone who has access to your business."

"Sure."

That was when it hit me that I didn't take my keys from Lexi's ass the other day. That bitch could be the one behind everything. I didn't say that to the police officer though. After they took their report, they left.

It wasn't shit they could do. The funny thing was, I had cameras up in the shop, but they were disabled. Mel and Bianca were the only two who knew about that.

I watched as the police pulled off. I locked up the shop and got in my car. I pulled off in a haste, pulled up to that bitch's house and parked on the other side of the road. I then grabbed my gun from the glove compartment and put it in my purse. I ran up her driveway and rang the doorbell. I didn't expect her to let me in, but I knew she would get upset if somebody kept ringing that bell. So, I rang it some more and then stood to the side.

"Man, who the fuck's ringing my shit like that?" she yelled as she swung the door open with an attitude.

I pushed that bitch with all my might. She fell backwards and I slammed the door behind me, locking it.

"You, stupid bitch. What you doing?" She got back on her feet and tried to lunge at me.

"Bitch, back the fuck up!" I pointed the gun in that bitch's face.

"Are you fucking serious Bianca? You're willing to risk going to jail behind some dick?"

Bap! Bap! Bap! I smacked the shit out of that bitch with the butt of the gun. I was way past reasoning. I was feeling homicidal right about now.

"Bitch, you think this is over a nigga. Nah, fuck that bitch. I know you went up in my shop and fucked it up. See, it's one thing to fuck with my nigga, but when you start fucking with my livelihood, that's when you really have a problem, hoe."

"Bitch, I ain't did shit to you, but fuck that. I'ma beat the fuck outta you." That bitch grabbed me and pushed me into the wall. I lost my balance and the gun flew out of my hand. That bitch started throwing blows. I started blocking them. That bitch was no match compared to the rage that I was feeling. I snatched that hoe by the hair and started pounding her face. It was blow for blow and I wasn't letting up. I heard that bitch's baby crying and that made her lose her focus. I let that hoe go and reached for my gun.

"Don't move bitch! I should blow your motherfucking brain out all over this floor! You have no idea who you fucking with bitch," I said while trying to catch my breath.

"Go ahead and pull the trigger bitch! Show me you ain't pussy," she teased.

I aimed the gun at that hoe's head! I took two steps closer to her and put my hand on the trigger. My children's faces flashed in front of me. "You lucky bitch! You ain't even worth the bullets. Nah bitch, I'ma watch you lose everything in your life." I turned, backed out of her house, ran down the driveway and jumped into my car with tears rolling down my face as I sped away.

I dashed into my house and straight into my room. I didn't want to explain what was going on to my aunt. I loved her to death, but right about then, I didn't want to hear shit from anyone. I turned my phone off, pulled the cover over my head and started crying a river. I released all my emotions and soaked my pillow with tears.

I heard a knock at the door, but I ignored it. However, it didn't let up any. I got up with a bad attitude. Those kids better get the fuck on and leave me alone right now.

"What is it?" I yelled.

"Ma, the police downstairs. I been knocking on the door," Melvin Jr. said.

"What? Police for who? Your daddy ain't here no more."

"They asked for you ma."

I walked down the stairs and opened the door.

"Yes, hello. My son said y'all are looking for me?"

"Ma'am are you Bianca Brown?"

"Yes, I am." In that second I regretted answering that, because I had a feeling something was about to pop off.

"Ma'am, please step outside. We have a warrant for your arrest."

"Arrest for what? I ain't did shit," I said with an attitude.

The police officer took several steps toward me and grabbed my arm. "Please turn around. You're under arrest for simple battery on Alexis..."

"Why y'all taking my mama?" My son ran outside.

"You better get yo' ass back in the house. Go get your auntie and let her know what's going on.

He looked at the police with his fists balled up. "Go now!" I yelled.

The last thing I needed was for them to hurt my damn baby. I was well aware of all the police brutality that was taking place against young black people. He saw the seriousness in my eyes and ran in the house.

A few seconds later my auntie came running out of the house. "What the hell is going on out here. Why's my damn baby in handcuffs?"

"Ma'am, please, step back. We are taking her to the local precinct. You can call down there for more information."

"Auntie, I will call you as soon as I get a bond. Go back in the house and lock the door."

They hauled me down the driveway and into the police car. I sat back there angry as fuck. I knew I'd beat that hoe's ass, but as bad as she claimed to be, I had no idea that bitch would call the fucking police and press charges. I should've left a hole in that old, stupid bitch's fucking face.

I was taken in front of the magistrate. She gave me a $10,000 bond. I was searched, fingerprinted and booked. I called my aunt to let her know how much my bail was. I also saw a bail bondsman's number on the wall when I was using the phone. She was hysterical, but I told her I needed her to quit all that damn crying and call the bondsman, so my ass could get the hell up out of jail.

They moved me to a cell that smelled just like stale urine, stinking ass and sweaty balls all mixed up together. I started gagging soon as I got in there. *This can't be life*, I thought. I had no idea how those bitches could be running in and out of jail. I took a seat at the edge of the filthy bench. I used my sweatshirt to cover my nose. Reality sank in that I was locked up behind a nigga. I hoped my babies were alright, especially my son. I didn't mean for him to see that. I felt like shit that I allowed myself to snap like that.

I sat there waiting impatiently. Every time I heard a sound, or the guards moving around, I jumped up only to be disappointed. It was three hours later and I still hadn't heard my name called. I was starting to get irritated. I knew it didn't take that damn long to post bond. Shit, when Mel got locked up numerous times, I was on it and that bum didn't have to sit in jail for hours.

"Bianca Brown." I opened my eyes and jumped up off the bench. I knew I heard my name, but I didn't see anyone. Shit, I realized that I had dozed off.

"Bianca Brown, you got bond. Let's go."

Those words were like a melody to my ears. She didn't have to tell me twice. She unlocked my cell and I walked out with her, almost running over her. That was how excited I was to get up on out of there. I met the bondsman and my auntie in the front. I signed the papers as he explained the rules of my bond. I thanked him and we left.

I got in the car and let out a long sigh. I was happy to be out of that hell hole. I could still smell that piss on my clothing. I couldn't wait to get in the house, so I could scrub that shit off me.

"What the hell happened today? I called up there and they were talking 'bout you assaulted somebody."

"Auntie, that bitch Lexi messed my shop up, so I beat that ass. I just didn't know the bitch would press charges."

"And who is this person? Is she a friend of yours?"

"She used to be."

I wasn't in the mood to explain all that shit. I was hungry, tired and most of all, angry. Hate filled my heart for Mel, because if it wasn't for him, none of that shit would be happening.

When I got home it was late and the kids were already in bed. I peeped in, but didn't bother to disturb them. I was mentally drained.

"Hey baby, I'm about to lay down, but if you need me just holla. Bianca remember, God won't give you more than you can bear my child. Stop fighting those people. Let God deal with them on his own time."

"Thanks auntie. Love you."

I walked in my room and then it hit me that I had not spoken to Jarvis. *Where is my damn phone?* I thought. It was on my bed where I had left it. I grabbed it and remembered that I'd turned it off earlier when I was crying. I hurried up and turned it on.

I grabbed my towel and then walked into the bathroom. I got into the tub and started strolling to see what calls I'd missed. I saw three missed calls from Melvin's ass. Surprisingly it was the first time that nigga had called my phone since he got caught sneaking up in there.

I also saw that my boo had been calling me and he sent texts messages to let me know that he was worried about me. I hurriedly dialed his number.

"Damn yo' Where you been? You got a nigga worried and shit."

"Man, you ain't goin' believe this shit. I was locked up."

"Stop playing yo. That ain't nothing for you to be joking about."

"I'm dead ass serious. I just got bonded out."

"And I'm just finding out? Man, what the fuck happened. Better yet, fuck that. You at the house? I'm on the way."

He didn't give me a chance to respond. He just hung up in my face. I wished I didn't say anything, but I had to tell him what was going on with me. I put the phone down on the bathroom floor and got up to turn the shower on. I had planned on taking a long bath, but he was on his way and I had no idea how close he was. I washed my body carefully, determined to get that stinking smell off my skin. The next day I would take my weave out and wash my hair. I just hope I never had to go back to that hell hole. I stood under the shower and let the water beat down on my skin.

I got out and oiled down. The wonders that a good moisturizer could do to the skin, especially during the cold weather. I threw on a pair of sweat pants and a T-shirt. I was going to meet him outside, because my aunt and the kids were there and I didn't want to bring him in without having a talk with the kids. True, they were sleeping, but I didn't want to risk them waking up. It wasn't the proper timing.

I watched him pull into the driveway like a mad man. I grabbed my fleece, threw it over me and flew outside just before he exited his vehicle. I jumped in on the passenger side.

"Yo', what's good witcha? And what, a nigga ain't welcome in the crib no more?"

"No, it's not that. The kids and my aunt are in there and before I just up and bring another nigga in their lives, I need to sit them down and talk to them. I just told them that me and their daddy are separated, so it would definitely be too soon to tell them about you."

"So, what happed? What you get locked up for?" I could tell he was bothered.

"This morning, I stopped by the shop and saw that somebody had fucked up everything. Only two people had keys to my shop and that was Mel and Lexi. So, I went to Lexi's house and beat that ass."

"Y'all homegirls right? Why would you think it was her and not that fuck nigga?"

"Because I recently found out that they might be fucking around with each other. The day I visited her in the hospital he was there. I stopped by her house when she got home. His car was parked outside, but his ass was hiding when I went in."

"Yo' shawty, let that nigga and that bitch go. I know you and the nigga got history and shit, but that nigga is a bitch. Let his ass go before I be forced to body his ass," he said in a serious tone.

I looked at him. He was no longer Jarvis the business owner, but Jarvis Coleman the thug. He wasn't in any casual wear. As a matter of fact, he had on sweatpants, Timbs and a fitted cap. He was looking a straight street king.

"I'm not fooling with him, but you know we got kids and shit. Regardless of what we go through, his kids need him."

"When you filing the divorce papers?" He turned to look at me.

He caught me off guard with that question. I'd thought about it since that nigga put his hands on me, but had yet to go see a lawyer. I really didn't want to, because the truth was, that nigga kept his money separate. The only thing we had together was the house.

"You know, I plan on doing it soon. So much happened with you getting shot and everything, I didn't have any time to really handle my business."

"Well, I'm outchea now, so you need to handle your shit before that nigga and that bitch lose their lives behind it. Listen Bianca, I play about a lot of things, but I don't play 'bout my money and my bitch. I go to war behind mine, for real."

"Anyway, enough about me. How you feeling? I hope you ain't running around already?"

"I feel good for real. I hit the gym earlier, trying to get my strength back."

"Well, I know you're eager to get back out there, but please take it easy babe."

"I got you. Now, come over here and give yo' man a hug."

I was happy he said that, because I needed a hug from him. After our hug, I sat in his lap. We started kissing passionately. I held his head and showed my man how much I missed him. He started fondling my breasts. Damn, my pussy started throbbing. I wanted to fuck him.

"Damn bae, I want you bad," he whispered in my ear.

"I want you too, boo." I wiggled on his dick, which I could feel poking me.

"Come spend the night with me."

I thought about it, I had to go. As much as I wanted to be dicked down, I needed some me time. I needed to get my mind right and my emotions under control.

"I'ma need to take a rain check babe."

"You sure about that, 'cause I think you want this pipe. He started pulling my sweatpants down.

"Boo stop. We're outside remember?"

"Come on boo. Sit on it real quick."

My mind was telling me no, but I was horny as fuck and my pussy was controlling my thoughts. I helped him ease my sweatpants down, pulled my panties down and straddled him. I took my time sliding down his pipe.

"Awee," I groaned out loud as his dick touched my inner soul. He grabbed my hips and pulled me down on every inch of his manhood. A few minutes before, I was stressed out and had the world on my shoulder, but his dick was taking me on a ride of pure bliss. I closed my eyes, threw my hair back, tooted my ass up, leaned forward and rode that dick like my life depended on it.

"Damn baby, work that pussy," he said as slapped me on the ass.

That sound only excited me more. I grinded and slow wined on that dick. You couldn't tell me I was not from one of those islands.

"Damn, oh shit. Ughhhh, ughhhh," he groaned as he pulled me down further on his dick

I started trembling as my insides erupted like a volcano and all my juices exploded on his dick. At the same time his juices were shooting up inside of me. He held me tight for a few minutes without any words. "I love you shawty," he whispered in my ear.

"Boy whatever. Oh, my God. I can't believe you got me out here fucking."

"Man, we grown as fuck. Plus, I was fiending for some pussy and not just any pussy, but this pussy right here." He massaged my wet pussy.

"Boy, stop." I pulled my panties up and then my sweatpants. They felt sticky and I would have to wait until I got inside to clean off.

We sat there talking for a little while longer and then I decided to go in. I was tired, plus I needed to take another shower.

"A'ight babe, I need to go in the house. I will call you after I finish taking a shower."

"A'ight shawty. Look, before you go, I want you to know e'erything's gonna be a'ight. Quit worrying about that fuck nigga. All you got to say is the word and I will body that nigga."

"Jarvis, I wish you'd quit saying that. He is the father of my kids, so I don't want him dead. I just want him out of my life."

"A'ight yo'. Hit my line when you finish. I'm about to take my ass to the house, take something for this pain and kick back."

I gave him a hug and got out of the car. I looked around and walked in the house. I prayed that no one was up, so I could just sneak in. I went in the bathroom and took a quick shower. Damn, I let him bust in me without being on any kind of protection. Fuck it. I was too worried about everything else to be thinking about some shit like that.

CHAPTER SIXTEEN

Lexi

I wanted to beat that bitch's ass, but I still wasn't feeling my best. I was mad as fuck after that hoe left. I tried calling my sister's phone, but it went straight to voicemail. Damn where the fuck was that bitch when I needed her? I sat on the couch, but then it hit me. That bitch had just assaulted me. I grabbed my cellphone and dialed 911. Normally, I didn't fuck with the police, but desperate times called for desperate measures. Trust me, it was urgent.

I waited for the police to come and filed the police report. After they left, I was pleased that they were going to lock her ass up. I could only imagine that bitch's face when they put those cuffs on her. I knew her ass was going to be crying and pleading for mercy.

I waited a few hours and then I called the jail. Sure enough, the police did exactly what they said they were going to do and picked her up. I felt relieved that they had that bitch in custody. My phone started ringing, which interrupted my few minutes of happiness. It was my boo and I was happy to hear his voice.

"Aye yo', you know who might've fucked Bianca's shop up?"

"Melvin, honey, what are you talking about?"

"Yeah, one of my niggas told me somebody went up in her shit and fucked everything up."

"Well, you know how Bianca loves going off on people. Shit, it could be anybody. You said she was fucking with a young nigga. Dude might have a woman, or something."

"Yeah, I thought about all that, but you know she had that alarm on at the shop."

"Well, what the fuck you asking me for? I ain't been nowhere, but in this house with my damn child.

Shit, who knows? That bitch got enemies every damn where."

"Man, calm down. I was just asking. You know that bitch goin' automatically think it was me. You know her ass love the police and shit."

"I know babe. Nah, I don't know who did that shit, but as cold as it sounds, that bitch deserves every bit of that shit. I know that's your wife and shit, but fuck her."

"You right bae. Fuck her. A'ight I got a few more runs to make and then I'll be there."

"Love you."

He hung the phone up without responding. Hmm, maybe he didn't hear me.

CHAPTER SEVENTEEN

Bianca

I jumped out of the bed, damn, I looked at the time. It was 7:45 am, and I had to be in court for my preliminary hearing. I was so tired that I didn't have a chance to contact a lawyer before I went in there to face the judge. I had never been in trouble before and was really nervous. I took a shower and got dressed.

My aunt was already in the kitchen when I walked downstairs. The strong aroma of coffee hit my nose as I walked into the kitchen.

"Good morning baby. How did you sleep?"

"You know I have so much on my mind. I barely got any sleep. I have court this morning, so I'm about to go."

"Oh child. Do you want me to get dressed and go with you?"

"No auntie. Just stay with the kids. I got this," I tried to assure her, even though I was as nervous as fuck.

"Alright. Well, call me if anything goes wrong."

I walked over and hugged her. "Auntie, this is just a prelim. I'll be fine."

After I drank a cup of coffee and ate a bagel, I brushed my teeth and was out the door.

Soon as I got in the car, the phone started ringing.

"Hey babe."

"Yo', you good? Do you need me to come wit' you this morning?"

"No, I'm good. I'm on my way now."

"You sure, 'cause you know I don't mind?"

"I know boo, but I got it. I will call you as soon as I leave out of there."

"A'ight yo'! Love you."

"Love you too." That was like my first time saying it back to him.

After he got off the phone, I took a few minutes to think about what I'd just said to him. I kind of shocked myself, because I vowed I would never love another man after Mel. It was hard not to love Jarvis. Other than the lies he told me about his career, he had been nothing short of great. He catered to my every need, he was respectful, his tongue game was sharp and he had that bomb ass dick. *Lord what else can I ask for,* I thought.

I sat waiting for the judge to enter the court room. I was no stranger to the courtroom, but never was I the accused. I logged on to FB to ease my mind a little.

"All rise. This court is now in session. The honora ble Judge Freewalt is presiding. Please be seated."

"Your honor, first up is docket number 67580. Defendant, Bianca Brown is charged with assault and battery."

"How do you, plea Mrs. Brown?"

"Not guilty your honor."

There was no way my black ass was going to plead guilty to shit. It was my word against that bitch's. All I needed was a bomb ass lawyer who could help me beat this case.

"Do you have a lawyer, or do you need the state to assign a lawyer for you?"

"I have to seek council your honor."

"Well in that case, we will have a continuance. You will be notified of your next court date."

I was dismissed and walked out of the court room. My heart was beating mighty fast, because that was my first time in front of a judge. I had to calm myself down as I exited the courthouse.

***

I finally got myself together to call the insurance company and report the damage to my store. I knew that they would cover most things, but I was hoping they'd cover everything. They told me they would send out an adjuster the next morning. Even though I had beat that bitch's ass and had got locked up, I still didn't feel any better. I'd busted my ass putting my business together and making a name for myself in the community. To see someone come in and destroy that had definitely put a dent in my heart. I also knew that I couldn't sit around and mope. I drove down there and put a sign on my door, letting my clients know that we had an emergency and would be back open in no time. I had some loyal clients and could only hope that they hung in there with me.

After I got home, I sat my ass down and Googled lawyers in my area. The judge set a date for me to go back to court and I had to make sure I have a lawyer to represent me that day. I was pretty sure that bitch was going to show up to testify against me. I now knew that she was no friend of mine, but an enemy who pretended like she was, so she could get close to my husband. I had so many questions that I needed answers to. Not that it was going to solve anything, but more so satisfy my curiosity. With me not talking to Mel and that scary bitch not telling me what I needed to hear, I was really aggravated.

***

I decided to cook dinner that evening. I'd been slacking on my parental duties lately and needed to tighten up a little. I decided to go all out and cook their favorite, which was roast and potatoes. It also gave my aunt a break from the kitchen. I swear, that lady had been cooking ever since she came. We sat at the table, laughing and talking like old times, although I noticed that my son was unusually quiet.

"You a'ight Junior?" I quizzed.

"Yeah, I just wish dad was here. Ma, why can't you let him come back home? I mean, you still love him, right?" He stared me dead in the eye.

I was definitely thrown off by his question. Everybody at the table turned their attention to me, I guess waiting for a response. I placed the fork down.

"I already told you what was going on between us. Daddy can't come back here. You don't get it right now, but you will one day."

"Is it because of that dude you talking to? Is that why daddy can't come back?"

My face turned red and my blood started boiling. "What are you talking about little boy? Where did you get that from?"

"He got that from daddy! He be talking to him all the time when he's in his room!" Trisha shouted out.

I tried my best to calm myself down. So, that old petty ass nigga was going to feed my son some shit, because he was mad at me.

205

"Give me your phone little boy."

"Why ma? He's still my daddy, even if you want to be fooling around with another nigga."

I flew over that table and slapped the shit out of that little boy. "Watch your fucking mouth! You hear me! Don't you ever feel like you can say whatever the fuck you want to me."

"I hate you! I want to go live with daddy. Your slutty ways are why daddy left us."

After that I blacked out, wrapping my hands around that little motherfucker's neck.

"Bianca stop! Get off him," my auntie's voice sounded off in my unstable mind.

"Mommy stop! Don't get in trouble over him!" I heard my daughter scream.

I looked down at that little bastard and his face started turning purple. I saw tears coming out of his eyes as he tried to gasp for air. I let him go and got off him. Get your ass out of my fucking kitchen and put your damn phone on my dresser."

That little bastard got up, shot me a dirty look and ran out of the kitchen.

"Mommy, you ok?" my baby girl asked me. My aunt stood there looking like she was at a loss for words. "Yeah, I'm good," I said before I stormed out of the kitchen and dashed upstairs to my room.

I sat on the edge of my bed, still trying to bring my anger level down. I couldn't believe that nigga Mel was feeding my son all that bullshit. I grabbed my cell phone and dialed his number. His phone rang, but there was no answer. I dialed it three more times, because I was pretty sure he saw me calling him.

I grabbed my house keys and my purse. I knew where his ass was posted at most of the time. I was certain his low life ass wouldn't be that hard to find.

"Auntie, I'll be right back. Make sure his ass stays in this house until I come back."

"A'ight baby…Bianca, don't go out there and do nothing crazy!" she yelled, but I was long gone.

I jumped in my car and pulled off, burning tires. I did one hundred mph all through the city looking for a nigga. He wasn't at the first two places I checked. I pulled up at the spot that I knew for sure his ass might be at. I spotted his Range Rover and parked across the street. I saw that he had got his windows fixed. I jumped out of my car and busted into the supposed to be tire shop, that was really a cover up for a dope spot. I didn't see him right away, but I spotted his right-hand man.

"Yo', where Mel at?"

"Damn, that's you B. I 'ont know. I think he went on the run!" he said loudly.

I was no fool. I knew he was only doing trying to tip Mel's ass off. "Don't fucking play with me Corey! Get that nigga out here, now." I pulled out my gun and aimed it at him.

Two other niggas pulled their guns out and pointed them at me.

"Nah, y'all chill. This Mel's wife."

"B, chill out yo'. That nigga ain't here for real."

"Fuck that Corey. I said get Mel's ass in here now!" I pressed the gun to his chest. I wasn't sure what I was doing, but I knew I was on the edge and anything could happen.

"Sean, get Mel out here. Tell him, his old lady out here."

I saw he noticed that I wasn't fooling around. I didn't flinch. I kept the gun pressed against his chest.

"Damn, you can get that shit off me now, shawty."

I totally ignored his ass. I wasn't doing shit until he got Mel out there. A few seconds later Mel's ass emerged from behind the closed doors.

He walked up to me, looking annoyed as hell. I didn't give a fuck. "Man, what you doing?"

"We need to fucking talk nigga," I turned and addressed his ass.

"Man, come in here."

I didn't trust him, so I kept the gun in my hand with my finger still on the trigger. I was prepared for anything with that sneaky ass nigga.

He took a seat behind a desk. I stood there looking at that nigga acting like he thought I was there to chill with him.

"Yo', what the fuck you doing? Walking up in here like you lost your damn mind. Do you know those niggas are stone cold killers?"

"I don't give a fuck about you, or any of those fuck niggas. I came here to talk about the bullshit that you been feeding my motherfucking son."

"What you talking about Bianca? Damn, you trying to take my son away from me too?"

"Cut the bullshit out Mel. You're trying to turn my son against me by telling him I'm sleeping around and shit."

"Bianca, I know I've always kept it one hundred with my kids. So, this time ain't no different. My son asked me why you won't let me come back home and I told him, 'cause you got a little nigga."

"Did you forget to tell him about his God mama that you've been fucking and have a child with? Did you tell him how you fucked your family up over that bitch? Nah, I bet you didn't."

"My son and I share a lot and in due time I'll let him meet his little sister. Bianca, you do know I love you, and when we got married it was for better or worse, right? I don't want that bitch. She was just something to do."

"You know what Mel. I fucking hate yo' ass. You need to stay the fuck away from my kids. If you don't, I will do whatever it takes to protect them from you."

"Be mindful when threatening me Bianca. You know Melvin the husband, you have not met Melvin the killer." He winked at me.

"You might put fear in those niggas out there, but I know the real you. When you take that mask off, you ain't nothing but a punk who preys on women. You not a real nigga." I turned to leave.

He stood up. "By the way, how is your little nigga doing? I heard he out of the hospital. No worries." He walked up to me. "Next time you will be planning his funeral."

I took several steps back, trying to digest what he'd just said. "What do you know about that?" I looked at him with grit on my face.

"Man, go ahead on. Just know I don't want that fuck nigga 'round my children."

"Boy, fuck you! You can't tell me who to have, or not to have around my kids. I couldn't tell you where to slang that dick. If I find out that you had anything to do wit' Jarvis getting shot, I promise you I'ma come for you personally," I said without blinking.

"Get the fuck out before I let them niggas throw yo' ass out of here."

"Ha, ha, that's so like you. Always have to find somebody to do your dirty work. You just as weak as the bitch you fucking, nigga!" I spat in disgust.

"Bitch, don't ever threaten me! I don't give a fuck if you carry the same last name as me. I will body your ass! Now, get the fuck out bitch!" He stared into my eyes without blinking.

I was going to respond, but instead, I looked at the nigga and smiled. I walked out of the office and entered the front where all those niggas were sitting around. They got silent as soon as I walked up. I didn't say a word, but in my heart, I dared any one of them to say something, so I could snap on their asses.

I exited the building and placed the gun back in my purse. I walked to my car and got in. I didn't feel any better than when I walked in. Mel was still the same old stupid ass nigga that I married. Why did I think I could actually talk to him on a mature level? I swear, when I looked back, I had no idea what my dumb ass saw in him. What the fuck was I thinking when I stayed in that fucked ass marriage? I was fucking done. I cranked the car up and busted a U-Turn in the middle of the street. I was fuming with anger. What Mel said about Jarvis getting shot kept replaying over and over in my mind. Something about what he'd said did not sit well with me. The grin he had plastered across his face gave me chills. Could Mel be the one behind that horrific situation and if so, did he follow us to the movie theater?

My mind was flooded with all sorts of thoughts. I thought about calling my bae to let him know what I was thinking, but I really didn't have any proof. I mean, I knew what Mel had said, but I needed more out of him. My brain started working.

***

It had been days since my son and I had that altercation and I was feeling like shit that I'd handled it that way. I knew he was out of order when he said the things he said, but Mel had used him for his own personal gain. I wanted to talk to my child, but I didn't want him to think it was okay to talk to me the way he did. I lived by the motto, 'I brought you in this world and I'll take you out.' I needed a drink to calm my nerves.

I got up, went down to the kitchen and made a strong drink of Rum and Pepsi. I needed something to relax me a little. I sat on the stool drinking and just thinking about everything in my life. How could something that was once so good, turn out so bad. I

DEVOTED TO A STREET KING

was a devoted wife and a good mother. I was so blind that I didn't see everything slipping away from me.

CHAPTER EIGHTEEN

Lexi

Mel had been bothering me about sex lately. Although I'd tried to tell him to wait until after my six weeks' checkup, which was only a few days away. I was laying in the bed watching TV when he entered the room. "Hey babe," he said as he walked in.

"Hey you, you're in early."

"Yeah, shit's slow out there. Plus, those pigs out there three cars deep."

"Oh, ok. Well, I didn't cook. I ordered some pizza though."

He didn't respond. Instead, he walked off toward the bathroom. I wasn't going to lie, I was happy that the nigga was in the house early. Our daughter was sleeping for now, so I could cuddle up with my nigga and probably catch a movie.

He got out of the shower and walked out of the bathroom with only the towel wrapped around him. He got in bed and pulled me closer to him. "Come here bae."

I scooted closer to him. He started kissing on my neck and massaging my breasts. I was loving the sensations that I was feeling. I'd missed us getting it in on the regular and couldn't wait. I had that in-house dick and didn't have to worry about him going home to that bitch after we made love.

I was so caught up in my thoughts that I didn't notice him pulling down my panties until they were almost by my knees. "Stop babe. Remember, I can't have sex until after I get my checkup. You only got a few days to wait boo."

He sat up in the bed. "Mane, fuck that. I ain't tryna hear some shit that the white man invented. You my bitch, this my pussy and I'm tryna fuck." He tried prying my legs open.

"Stop, what is wrong with you?"

"What the fuck you mean. Are you fucking another nigga? Is that the reason why you 'ont want to give me the pussy?"

"Boy, shut the fuck up talking like that. I had your fucking baby. That's the reason why we ain't been fucking. So, go ahead with that foolishness, for real nigga."

He didn't respond. That nigga just pulled my underwear down and slid his hard, dry dick inside of him.

"Stop Mel. What are you doing? What is wrong with you? I've never seen you behave like this." I tried to understand what was really going on.

"Damn, open up babe," he said as he sank his dick deeper inside of me.

The smell of alcohol reeked through his pores. Tears gathered in my eyes as I felt violated. I had never been raped before, but that was how I was feeling right then. I closed my eyes as I tensed my body up.

"I know you loving it baby. Throw it on me boo," that fool whispered in my ear.

I didn't say a word. I just let him think in his fucking mind, that I was enjoying myself.

"Damn bae. This shit got tighter. It's gripping my dick."

God, please let that nigga stop.

"Aarrrggghhh! I'm about to bust. You back on the pill bae?

"Man, get up off me!"

He jumped off me and busted in his hands.

I jumped off the bed and ran to the bathroom. I sat on the toilet and started crying. I couldn't believe Mel had just done that to me. I guess I should've appreciated it, because he could've went out and fucked another bitch, but instead he came home to me. Fuck that. I didn't feel special.

I managed to get my crying under control. I jumped in the shower and took a quick rinse off. Still in my feelings, I wasn't in the mood to say a word to him. I got out the shower, put on a pair of pajamas and walked in the room. His ass was knocked out already. I grabbed a pillow and stormed out of the room. I laid on the floor in my daughter's bedroom. I knew she was going to be waking up in a few and God knows, I was tired as hell.

CHAPTER NINETEEN

Bianca

I was on my way to meet with a divorce lawyer that I found on the internet. I read the reviews about his firm and he seemed qualified. I pulled into the parking lot of the building. I parked, grabbed my purse and got out of the car. I walked to the front of the building and pressed the buzzer.

"Good morning. My name is Bianca Brown and I have an appointment with Attorney Laworski."

Good morning. Yes, he's expecting you."

"Mr. Laworski, your nine am appointment is here. Yes sir. He's ready to see you. Come with me."

I followed her through a huge door and into an office.

"Good morning Mrs. Brown. Please take a seat."

I took a seat and waited for him to finish with the stack of papers he was skimming through.

"Ok, I know from our brief conversation that you mentioned you want to file for divorce from your husband. Well, can you tell me a little about what brought you to this point."

I looked at that man. Was he serious? Where did I start? That nigga had lied, cheated, beat on me and some more shit.

Eventually, I was finished pouring my heart out and giving him all the reasons why I wanted to walk away from that piece of shit.

"Well, this should be easy. I can file for divorce based on infidelity. Also, you two don't have any assets together other than the house. Since you and the children live there, I'm going to ask the judge to grant the house to you. Also, I will ask for full custody of the children, because he's an unfit parent. This process won't be long. In the meantime, I think you need to secure a permanent order of protection against him. He seems like a dangerous man. You can never be too careful these days."

"Yes, I plan on doing that Monday morning. Thank you for everything."

'You're welcome. I'm going to get on this ASAP."

I left his office feeling relieved. It had been a long time coming and finally, I had the courage to walk away from that nigga. I used to say for years that I was going to leave, but deep down my ass was lying, for real. I loved that nigga and his dirty drawers and put up with a lot, because I believed his lies. A tear dropped from my eye as I thought about the past. I was a fucking fool, because my dumb ass was so in love that I was oblivious to the fact that he and my so called best friend were having a whole relationship behind my back.

***

I was so tired that I fell asleep on the couch. The ringing of a phone woke me up. I reached for my phone, which was on the coffee table. "Hello," I said without looking at the caller ID.

"Hey babe, I know you ain't sleeping," Jarvis said.

I sat up quickly. "No, I was just laying down for a few."

"Well, get yourself together. I'll be pulling up in about ten minutes."

"Huh, where are we going?"

"Woman, just do as I say. Dang, can you relax and let me be the nigga?"

"A'ight nigga, calm down," I said in a playful manner.

After he hung the phone up, I got up and went up the stairs. I brushed my teeth and washed my face. I wasn't sure where we were going, so I didn't bother to change out of the clothes that I had on. I applied a little make-up and lip-gloss before grabbing my purse. He was being all mysterious and shit. I smiled, because truthfully, I loved that shit.

I heard his car horn and rushed outside. I was too excited to see what that man had up his sleeve. Shit, the way I was feeling, I hoped it was something to get me out of my funk.

"Hey babe," he said as he kissed me and gave me a hug.

"Hey boo." I hugged him back and got in the car.

He pulled off without saying a word. I waited a few minutes and then spoke.

"So, babe what's going on? You seem to be in a good mood today."

"I am. The pain's not too bad today and I get to see my boo. What else can a nigga ask for?"

"I guess nothing else, right?" I laughed.

I saw that he wasn't going to budge, so I closed my eyes, listening to Kevin Gates's voice blasting through his speakers.

My mind kept wondering what he was up to. It was a little after two pm, so lunch was over. Maybe it was an early dinner, or something. I was driving myself crazy thinking about what that man had up his sleeve.

I felt the car stop. Opening my eyes, I looked up. He stopped at a house. I didn't recognize the area. "You coming with me, or you staying? I got to talk to my partner real quick."

I thought about just sitting in the car, but since he'd asked, I decided to tag along. I just hoped it wasn't any drug business, because this bitch did not want to be involved in any federal investigations.

I got out of the car and walked to the gate with him. I noticed that another car pulled up. He stopped and waited. An older, white man with a beard got out and walked up to us.

"Coleman, my man. Let's go inside. Hello ma'am." He nodded to me.

The man walked up to the house and opened the door. We followed him inside.

It was a nice ass mini mansion. "So, babe, do you like?" He turned to me and asked.

"Huh, are you talking to me?"

"Yeah, you."

"Well, it's nice from what I see. Let me see the rest of it." I walked around downstairs. It was like the designer had laid out each brick with a certain kind of style in mind. The kitchen was beautiful. From the marble counter top, to the large oven and the expensive stove, it screamed money from a mile away. I backed out of the kitchen and walked upstairs. There were four bedrooms and they were huge. The master bedroom's walk in closet was the size of another bedroom. The Jacuzzi was a sight to see. It was beautiful. I opened the doors that led to a balcony outside of the bedroom. It was beautiful, because there was a nice view of the city.

"So, do you like it woman?" Jarvis crept up behind me and asked.

"Yes, it is beautiful. Is this your friend's house?"

"Oh nah, but it's yours as soon as you tell me you want it."

I stood there stuck. I tried to replay what he'd just said to me. "Quit playing. I already have a house. I mean, it ain't this huge and beautiful, but it's ok."

"Nah, this is yours. That other house is what you and that nigga bought. You my woman now, so you need something much classier. So, woman is it a go?"

"Sure, yes. Oh, my God. Can you afford this?"

"Man, chill out. I told you I'm a street king. This ain't shit and yes, it is all yours."

Tears welled up in my eyes. I was too damn happy. It was the most beautiful thing anyone had ever done for me."

"Come on, let's go talk to that nigga."

We walked downstairs hand in hand. "So, Mr. Johnson, the lady said she loves it, so it's a go for me."

"The lady got taste. This house is beautiful and it is brand new. The neighborhood is also nice and the school system is one of the best in the county."

"That's great, because that's very important to me."

"Okay Mr. Coleman, let me go to the office and get all the paperwork together. Give me forty-eight hours at the most and you all can come into the office to sign the papers."

"Nah, take her number and call her when you're ready. She is the sole owner. You already got the numbers, so we're straight."

"Ten four, sir. Okay, ma'am, you will be hearing from me within two days."

'Thank you."

We left, and he stayed inside. I looked around the backyard and it was just as beautiful. It had an area where I could have cookouts and get together. I knew the house wasn't cheap. I wanted to ask how much it was, but I decided to keep quiet. I got in the car, then he got in and drove off. "Aye boo, I'm happy you liked it."

"Like is not the word, I love it. I just think we're moving a little too fast. I mean, the divorce isn't final and we've only been together for..."

He looked at me, pulled the car over and stopped. "Yo' B, what type of shit you on. Fuck that divorce! A piece of paper don't make, or break our relationship. You my motherfucking bitch. I don't give a fuck about no man-made piece of paper. I never feel comfortable coming over to the house that you and that nigga lived in anyways. You need to stop acting like I'm not your nigga yo'."

I could tell he was angry with me, so I chose my words carefully. "Babe, I know. All I'm saying is, I don't want you to go all out of your way to get me a house. I was going to sell my house and try to get another one."

"Well, Bianca if that's what you choose to do, then do that. Shit that one's yours too, so sell that shit if you want too. See, you so used to those fuck niggas that you can't recognize when a real nigga fucks with you." He started the car up and pulled off.

Those words stung my soul. Although I wanted to lash out against him, I kept it inside, because he was right. I remembered all the fake promises that Mel made to me before we got married. I learned from fucking with Mel that I could not depend on a man.

I remained quiet for the rest of the ride. I did not want to start a fight with him. I thought he was going to take me straight home, since he was so angry, but he pulled up to his house instead.

He got out the car and I sat inside pretending like I was on the phone.

"Man, come on and quit playing."

His tone was a little off, but kind of sexy. I loved how he was taking control. It was fine as long as he didn't start being disrespectful. I got out of the car and followed him in the house. He disappeared upstairs to his bedroom.

I hesitated about walking up the stairs, but why not? I was there already. Before I could knock on his bedroom door, it swung open.

"Damn, you act like you don't want to come in."

"If I didn't want to come in, I wouldn't be here," I said nonchalantly. Something was telling me to leave right then, because I didn't have time for the bullshit.

"Shit, you don't have to have an attitude. I just asked a simple question, so miss me with the attitude, or you can leave my shit." The nerve of that nigga. I swear, I couldn't go through it any longer with him.

"Fuck you Jarvis! I can't take your shit any longer. I'm out." I back peddled toward the door.

He came chasing after me, "Come on Bianca. Baby, I'm sorry. You know a nigga was missing you, that's all."

Tears fell from my eyes and down my face. That nigga had no idea all the shit that I'd been through with that nigga Mel and why it was so hard for me to trust another nigga.

"I can't do this! I just can't." I balled my fists tightly and started pounding on his chest.

"Baby, I love you." His heavy arms wrapped around me, "Bianca, you know you mean the world to me," he continued to whisper in my ear. Right then, I wanted to kill his ass. He made me so fucking sick. Ugh.

My tears were unbearable. I was having mixed feelings, because I loved him, but I was so scared to let him know that. He started kissing on my neck and then down to my shoulders. Damn, I was missing his affection, his touch, his scent and most importantly, his loving.

Don't give in girl, my inner voice said, but his kisses were so passionate. I felt his hands traveling up my shirt, rubbing my back. I couldn't resist his touch. My lips made their way to his neck and I planted soft kisses inside his earlobe. "I love you so much Jarvis." Now I found myself whispering in his ear.

All my tears were dried up. My heart had gone from being irritated with him, to professing my love. He was all I wanted and needed. I felt my bra unbuckle and my breath dropped down a few inches. He pulled up my shirt and my breasts flopped freely, breathing. He cuffed my breasts with his hands and started kissing on my nipples.

"No, oh God, I can't," I moaned out, "Oh, Lord." He was hitting my hot spot and his left hand was rubbing my clit. My pussy was on fire, throbbing, wanting some attention.

Stop tripping bitch, my inner voice whispered. I helped assist in unbuttoning my pants. My pussy needed something inserted in it; fingers, tongue, dick, I couldn't care less which order it was in, long as something was satisfying my needs.

"Bianca, I missed you baby," Jarvis growled as he continued sucking my breast. Fuck the small talk, I kept my mouth closed and guided his hands inside my panties and into my wetness.

"Oh, yes baby." His fingers were sliding in and out my wetness. My nipples were hard and his tongue twirled around them, causing my hormones to go crazy.

"Hmmm." I grinded my hips in rhythm.

"Oooooh, shit." He was driving me crazy, biting on my nipples, just the way I liked it. I started twirling my fingers around his ears. My body was totally relaxed as if it had a mind of its own.

He worked his way up my neck to my face, then my lips. Our tongues danced together. My pants were down to my ankles and my panties were just beneath my thighs. "Sssss, dammit man," I didn't have a hard time pulling his anaconda out of his shorts. I guided it into my wetness. He scooped me up and pinned my body against the wall. I wrapped my legs around his waist and my arms around his neck.

"Hmmmm," I moaned while his dick penetrated in and out my pussy. "Damn, this dick is so good." I started biting his neck to keep from moaning too loud.

"Fuck this pussy," I gasped between strokes.

The tip of his dick hit my clit continuously, which sent frequent shock waves through my body. I couldn't explain how I was feeling inside, but my body felt like it was melting. I had to catch my breath, because each thrust he took had me in la la land. "Yes, right there. Shit yes!" I let out a loud cry when a large shock wave erupted through my body and my juices flowed between my legs.

He got up off the bed and walked to the bedroom while I laid there, trying to catch my breath. This was what you called make up sex. All my anger towards him was gone and I was feeling love all over again.

"You a'ight babe?" he asked as he walked back into the room.

"Yes, I need to get my ass up." I got up and walked to the bathroom.

It was kind if surprising how clean his bathroom really was. Hmm, made me wonder if a woman was keeping his place tidy.

I was curious and there was only one way to find out. I walked out of the bathroom and he was fully dressed. I grabbed my underwear and put them on.

"Aye boo, can I ask you an honest question?"

"Yeah, whaddup?"

"Are you involved with anyone other than me? I mean, I know you're in the streets and street niggas have a certain reputation. Having plenty bitches is one of them."

"Yo, where is this coming from?"

"Just answer the question. I want to know. Scratch that, I need to know."

"Listen shawty, I'm a man and a boss. I see bitches e'eryday. Most of them throw pussy at me. Shit, a few might suck a nigga off, but ever since I met you, I've been trying not to entertain those bitches. My heart belongs to you."

"I just don't have time for no bullshit for real. I just got out of a fucked-up situation and definitely don't want to be in another one."

I finished getting dressed and turned to him. "Aye boo. The night that Mel walked in on us, was that the first time y'all crossed paths?"

He looked at me all strange. "What do you mean? I don't know that nigga."

"Oh ok, 'cause he's in the streets and now I know you are, so I thought you might've seen him around before."

"Nah B, I never laid eyes on that fuck nigga before and I hope that was the last time we ever cross paths."

"Well, you know, I went to see him the other day, because he's been feeding my son some bullshit."

"Did you? So, why am I just now hearing about this? You know that nigga is dangerous, so why the fuck you even going around him?"

240

"I was so upset after my son told me what he told him. I went to the spot I knew he'd be at. I swear, I was angry at him. I can't believe I actually laid with that man, much less married him."

So, why did you ask me if we met before?" He caught me off guard with that question.

I contemplated about lying, but quickly decided to be straight up with him.

"We got into a heated argument the day I went to see him and he said something about the shooting that kind of threw me off."

"Go ahead."

I went on to tell him what Mel said about the shooting. They were things that he should not have known. I knew that I didn't have any proof, but it had been bothering me since the day I walked out of his office.

Jarvis didn't say much. He just sat there listening attentively.

"You ready to go babe?" he asked without responding about what I just told him.

"Yup, I am."

He locked his house up and we got in his ride. He turned the music up loud, reached over and held my hand.

"Listen babe, don't tell anyone else what you just told me, a'ight?"

"I'm not, but don't you think we should go to the police?"

"Bianca, don't you ever mention going to the police no mo'. I ain't no rat and I don't deal with the law. In my world, we deal with niggas in the streets. It's death before dishonor."

I noticed, he was no longer the jovial guy that I met. He was more cold and calculated. I sat in my seat, wondering if I'd made the right decision. *God please show me a sign*, I thought as I leaned my seat back and closed my eyes.

CHAPTER TWENTY

Lexi

Melvin had been trying to make up for what he did to me the other night. He came home with flowers and even took me to the spa to get a facial, manicure and pedicure. I tried my best to stay mad at him, but I couldn't. I gave in to him and his demands. Every night he came home, he was beating the pussy up. It was as if I didn't just give birth to a baby. I guess the saying was true. That pussy was like an elastic band, because my shit was gripping that nigga's dick, almost suffocating it. Even my pussy was getting wetter. The other night, I thought I'd pissed on the bed, but when I checked it was all my juices flowing out.

I decided to cook some baked chicken and macaroni and cheese that night. Look now, I wasn't the best cook in the world, but shit that nigga was dicking me down so good, that I decided to try my hand. Shit, I even Googled some recipes and was ready to make it do what it do.

I put my baby in her swing, so she could watch her mama throw down for her daddy. It was amazing how she favored her daddy and unfortunately, she was starting to look like that bitch's daughter. If I had anything to do with it, my baby wouldn't be around their asses, especially after what that bitch did to me.

After I finished cooking, I decided to put the food in the oven so it would stay warm. It would be nice if he come home early, but I knew that wasn't going to happen. I bathed my baby, fed her and tucked her in her warm bed.

I decided to take a bath and relax my mind a little. I turned the music down low and closed my eyes, taking in the sweet melodies of Sade. I heard footsteps coming up the stairs. "Mel, is that you?" I hollered.

"Yeah, it's me."

My heart fluttered and I felt butterflies in my stomach. I was so happy that he was home early. Let me find out that nigga loved coming home to me and his daughter. I hurried and bathed, then rinsed off in the shower. I wrapped my robe around my body and walked into the room. I noticed he was not there. I walked down the stairs and saw him sitting in the living room in the dark. Instantly, I figured something was wrong. I entered with caution. "Hey bae, you a'ight?"

"Hell nah, I ain't a'ight. I need that bitch dead for real," he lashed out as he took a bottle of liquor to his head.

"What bitch?" I asked, which might've been a mistake.

"That bitch Bianca, what other bitch you think I'm talking about?"

I had no idea what triggered his latest tirade, but I was curious to know. I walked over to him, took a seat and started massaging his shoulder.

"What did that bitch do now boo?"

"That bitch done filed for a fucking divorce."

"Isn't that a good thing? I thought that was what you wanted?" I was confused as fuck. What was he bitching about?

"I don't give a fuck 'bout that bitch wanting a divorce, but that bitch want full custody of my kids. Fuck nah, that shit ain't happening. Over my dead body."

"What? Why do that bitch think you'll just walk away from your fucking kids like that?"

"Man, I 'ont know, but that bitch has no idea who the fuck she's playing wit'. On my dead pops, I will body that bitch."

I knew he was serious by his tone and how he was staring off into space. "Listen bae, calm down. We can come up with something." My mind was racing as I tried to come up with a plan to help my man out.

CHAPTER TWENTY-ONE

Bianca

After having second thoughts about taking the house, I decided to go ahead and sign the papers. I called the realtor and went down to the office to sign the papers. Everything was paid for, so he gave me the keys and the deed to the house. I was happy as hell once I pulled up to the house by myself. I didn't tell Jarvis that I was stopping by, because I needed a moment to myself. When I walked through the house, paying attention to every little detail, I was in tears. No one had ever given me anything. For that nigga to bless me like that, really made me emotional and grateful to him.

I took one last glance around, locked my door and walked back to my car. On my out of the neighborhood, I looked around to the beautiful estate that would become my new home. From what I could see, it was an upper-class neighborhood that seemed pretty quiet.

"Hello," I answered the phone without looking at the caller ID.

"Mrs. Brown, this is Attorney Laworski. I just wanted to inform you that your husband was served with the divorce papers."

"Oh yeah, thank you so much."

"So, this shouldn't be a long process at all. Mrs. Brown, please be careful."

"Thank you so much. And don't worry, I will."

After he hung the phone up, I experienced a sense of relief. I was happy that it was all finally coming to an end. I could finally get my freedom and my last name back. It was the time for me to have a talk with the kids again, since we would be moving and the divorce would be officially over soon.

I pulled into my garage and got out the car. I walked upstairs and right away, I smelled something good. It didn't take long for me to realize that it was my auntie in the kitchen working her magic. "Hmmm, you have this kitchen smelling like Martha Stewart's kitchen up in here."

"Child, stop your foolishness! Martha is a white woman and damn sure can't have no kitchen smelling like this. Your grandma taught your mama and me to season the hell out of some meat. Oh, how I miss your mama." Her voice cracked sadly.

Yes, I knew the feeling. My mama was my best friend. I learned she was beaten up to the point where she was in a coma. A few months later, she was gone. I remembered the day my auntie picked me up from school. I knew then that something terrible had happened. That was the day that I lost a piece of my soul and had to grow up fast. My auntie stepped up to the plate and took us in, but all the love that my aunt tried to provide us with, could never replace my mama's love.

I felt my eyes watering, so I quickly refocused my thoughts. Auntie walked over to me and placed her hands on my shoulders.

"I know you miss her, but if my dear sister was here today, she'd be so proud of the woman that you've become. I know because I'm proud of you, my dear. It ain't always been easy, but you pulled yourself together and now look at you?"

I smiled at her and was about to respond, but I heard the doorbell. "Are the kids home?"

"Yes, they are upstairs."

"I wonder who the hell that is. It better not be those people trying to sell pies again. I told their asses about ringing my damn bell." I stormed off to go check those motherfuckers again.

I unlocked the door and opened it. There was a woman and two uniformed police officers standing to the side. My stomach felt queasy and my palms started sweating.

"Good evening. How can I help you?"

"Hello are you Mrs. Brown?" The woman asked.

"Yes, that's me, who are you and what do you want?" I was starting to get irritated.

"We're with the department of social services and we have an order to remove your two children from your home, pending an investigation of abuse, child neglect and child endangerment. Here is the court order." She shoved a piece of paper in my hand.

I leaned against the door, trying to give myself support, because I felt like I was about to faint.

"What the fuck are you talking about lady? Who is getting abused?" I looked at her, then at the officers.

"Ma'am, all of the information is in the order and you have a court date on Wednesday in front of a judge. Where are the children? We have to take them."

"Take them? What do you mean? My kids are not being abused. You can talk to them. See for yourself." I started crying.

By then the officers were pushing past me and into my house. "What's going on here?" I heard my auntie ask.

"Ma'am, please step back. Where are the children?"

By then the kids must've heard the commotion and they were heading down the stairs.

"Ma, what's going on?" My baby girl ran towards me, but was stopped in her tracks by one of the police officers.

"Get your hands off me." She started fighting back.

"Calm down before I put these cuffs on you," he said as he tried restraining her.

"Get off my damn child. I swear, you are going to hear from my fucking lawyer." I tried to get to my child, but my path was blocked. I thought about swinging on those motherfuckers, but I knew it would turn out all wrong and I didn't want my kids to be caught up in that shit.

"Listen baby, just go with them. I promise mama will be there to get you." Those were the hardest words that I had to say to my child. I wanted to reach over and wipe her tears, but I couldn't. I turned to my son to say the same comforting words, but he looked at me, shot me a dirty look and turned his head.

It was as if he took a knife and sliced through my heart. I forced the tears back. They took my kids out of the house and there was not a damn thing I could do about it. I fell to the ground as I watched them pull off with my life line.

"Baby c'mon, we goin' get to the bottom of this. They can't just walk up in here and take your damn kids with no reason. This is crazy," she said as tears started falling down her face.

I got up, ran to the kitchen, grabbed my purse and stormed upstairs. I locked my bedroom door and fell to the floor. My heart was aching and my head was pounding. What the fuck were these people talking about? Other than the situation that had happened between my son and I a few weeks ago, nothing else happened. I was not a perfect mother, but those kids were my damn life.

I grabbed my phone and dialed Mel's phone.

"Yo'!"

"What did you do? You got my kids taken away from me, you bastard!" I yelled as loud as I could.

"Shawty, you need to calm down. You don't want them to think you crazy too."

"You know what Melvin, you're weaker than I thought. What lies did you make up? You know damn well my kids are my life."

"Shit, that may be true back in the day, but now you're too busy chasing dick. You're barely home with the kids and beating on them is so not cool. Shawty, I never thought you was the kind to choose a fuck over your kids, but shit, it looks like I ain't really know you."

"I fucking hate you. You're a weak ass nigga. Your bitch of a mother should've swallowed your ass instead of getting pregnant with you."

"Bitch what? You thought you were going to put me out of my shit, press bogus charges on me and then bring your nigga up in my shit and nothing happened? Fuck nah, I really want to body your ass, but I decided to make you suffer slowly, until you kill yourself." Before I could respond, he hung the phone up.

I tried calling back, but his phone kept going to the voicemail. "You fucking coward!" I yelled out.

I was angry, hurt and desperate. I dialed his bitch's number, but her shit just rang and rang. I threw my phone across the room and buried my head in my hands. I got on my knees and start praying to God. I needed him more than ever.

***

I couldn't sleep so I just paced the floor. I felt like I was losing my mind. I tried to figure out how that nigga could go from loving me to hating me so much. He was behaving like I'd violated him when he was the one carrying me.

The phone continued ringing for what seemed like a million times, and I knew it was Jarvis. I wanted to get on the phone and cry to him, but I was feeling some type of way, because Mel insinuated that I was choosing dick over my children.

"Bianca, that fella is here to see you." My aunt knocked on the door.

"Why? What? Why did you let him up in here?"

"You need all the support you can get. I talked to him through the door and realized it was him. You need him."

I opened the door and Jarvis was standing there. I didn't recall saying anything, I just collapsed into his arms. I felt safe now that he was there.

CHAPTER TWENTY-TWO

Lexi

I was shocked when Mel asked me to help him file abuse papers against Bianca. I mean, I didn't fuck with the bitch, but taking her kids was far from what I was thinking. I tried talking that nigga out of that bullshit.

"Listen babe, you really don't want to take the kids from their mama, do you?"

"What the fuck you mean shawty? That bitch ain't no mother to my son and all she can teach my daughter to do is suck dick, for real. Shit, now we can really be a family; you, me, baby girl and her brother and sister."

The bread that I was eating was kind of stuck in my throat. Who the fuck told that nigga that I was a willing participant in that bullshit? I knew I loved the nigga, and wanted him and I to be a family, but that bitch's children were never included in my plan.

"You a'ight? Why the fuck you looking like that?"

I tried to pull myself together fast. "Oh, nothing. A tension headache just hit me," I lied.

There was no way I could tell him that his kids were not welcome in our little family. At least not right now anyways.

"Oh a'ight, 'cause your man needs your support on this one. You know I'm a street nigga, so I need some help filing these papers."

He reached over the table and grabbed my chin. "I can count on you, right?"

He kissed me on the lips and looked me in the eye.

"You know, I got you boo. I say we got work to do then."

"That's more like it babe."

My insides were doing flips. I was irritated as hell, but I held my composure and started Googling information. Within an hour, I had all the information on how to get children removed from an abusive home. I gave the info to him and sat there as he called up the department of child services.

"Now, let's sit back and see how long it's gon' take those people to go up in there and snatch my children. See, after they do that, they ain't goin' have no choice but to give me full custody at the divorce hearing," he chuckled.

It was something about that laugh that made my body shiver. Maybe it was the fact that he mentioned that Bianca had the kids around drugs and illegal activities. To watch and see him make that up, was very alarming. Oh well, that wasn't my beef, so I kept my nose out of it.

***

It was time for me to get myself back into the work field. Mel was holding everything down, but I was too independent to depend one hundred percent on a nigga. I remembered him saying that he'd help me to open my own shop, so I was ready to take him up on that offer.

The good thing was, my sister boyfriend's brother got all my shit out of the shop before he vandalized it. So, I had most of my important tools that I needed to start over. I could tell he did a pretty good job by the pictures that I requested that he send to my phone. I knew exactly where to hit that bitch; right in her motherfucking pockets. I bet you her ass still hadn't fixed that shop back up. Oh well, back to my situation. I needed to get my own shop and hire a few stylists and shut the city down. I wanted my shop to be the 'talk of the town'.

My phone started ringing. I grabbed it and noticed it was Mel. "Hey babe."

"Boo, I told you that they was goin' get the kids from outta there!" he yelled into the phone.

"Wait, what are you talking about and how you know that?"

"Man, don't worry 'bout how I know that. Just know that I should be getting a phone call soon and bringing my kids home."

What the fuck did that nigga mean by home? How the fuck did he think we were all going to squeeze into a little, two-bedroom apartment? Fuck, my baby wasn't sharing a room with anybody.

"Listen babe, let me call you back. That's the daycare on the other line," I lied.

"A'ight bet."

I was anxious, to get him off the fucking phone. Matter of fact, I needed a fucking drink. Yes, it was only eleven am, but my ass needed a something to calm my nerves. I went into the kitchen where Mel had some vodka and poured myself a glass. I wasted no time drinking it down. I had a feeling my sanity was about to explode.

CHAPTER TWENTY-THREE

Bianca

My heart was heavy as I pulled into the parking lot of the DeKalb County Courthouse. I'd prayed and prayed that God would intervene on my behalf. I knew I'd done some shit in my younger days, but I was no longer that person. I couldn't really see the reason behind all the shit that was happening to me. For a nigga to make up bogus charges against me was fucking ridiculous.

I whispered another prayer to God, before I exited my car. I dabbed my eyes, trying to stop the flow of tears that were constant since they removed my kids from my house. I walked into the courtroom and searched the docket for the courtroom that I need to be in. I had no idea what the hearing was about, but I was ready to let that damn judge have it.

The courtroom was empty when I entered it. It was still early, so I sat down trying to calm myself down. My aunt had offered to come with me, but like I told her and Jarvis, I needed to handle everything on my own.

After twenty minutes, I heard the courtroom door open. A woman and a man entered. I wanted to know who the hell they were. "Good morning, are you here for the hearing for Brown?"

"Good morning, yes and who are you?"

"I'm their mother. Where are my babies?"

"Your children are in the care of the state right now. The judge will decide if they will stay in state custody, go back to you, or to the father."

"What? I never abused my damn kids. How is this possible?"

"Calm down Mrs. Brown. We were assigned by the court to represent the children and then give our recommendation."

"Lady, no disrespect, but just because you have a degree doesn't mean y'all get to decide what is best for my kids. If you talked to them, I know they told you I never abused them. That's what they said right?"

"I'm sorry, but we have to give our findings to the judge. I suggest if you're trying to get your children back to tone your attitude down a little bit."

I wanted to snap that bitch's head off her body. It took everything in me to walk away. A dude entered the courtroom, I assumed, he was representing the state. I took a seat and put my head down. I whispered one last prayer to God.

***

All Rise, the Honorable Judge Dixon presiding over case Brown vs. the state of Georgia. You may be seated.

"Thank you, Officer Bells."

"Your Honor this is an emergency removal proceeding."

"Your honor, we have reasonable cause to believe that the children were at substantial risk of harm, or in surroundings that present an imminent risk of harm. An immediate removal was necessary pending this court's proceedings."

"Are the parents present?"

"I'm the mother, your honor." I walked up to the front.

"Your honor may I speak?"

"Go ahead."

"We have evidence to show that the mother abused her son and not only that, but here are pictures of the mother engaging with a well-known drug dealer who has been on the federal watch list for some time now. Not only that, but this gentleman has frequented the home where the mother and her children live."

"Your Honor, I have no idea what this man's talking about. All of those lies were made up by my soon to be ex-husband. Those charges are bogus your honor. I am a good damn parent. Talk to their teachers, their coaches and their doctor!" I yelled.

"Please calm down Mrs. Brown. I understand you're upset, but this is about your children. A complaint was made and we have to follow up and make sure the children are safe."

"Your Honor, no disrespect, but these are my damn kids. To y'all they are just a number. I carried them for nine months. I took care of them their entire lives. So, who gives y'all the power to just come in and disrupt my home? Where the fuck are y'all when they're hungry, or need clothes and shelter, huh?" The tears started flowing and my emotions came pouring out.

"Mrs. Brown please be quiet, or I will hold you in contempt of court!" the judge yelled.

I was too far gone to stop now. I continued letting them know how bogus that shit really was.

"Bailiff, please place Mrs. Brown under arrest."

"Noooooooo your honor. I just want my kids back. I swear I just need my kids," I pleaded as the officer placed the cuffs on me and dragged me out of the courtroom.

***

Reality set in, as I sat in that cell. That was my second time being locked up within months. I wiped the tears away as they fell on my arm. I had to sit in here for twenty-four hours with four more to go. My mind was speeding as all sorts of thoughts filled my head.

I was happy to be walking out of that jail. I instantly spotted Jarvis's car. He must've spotted me too, because he got out and greeted me.

"Get in." He wasn't his old cheery self.

I got in the car and he pulled off. After a few blocks, he turned the music down.

"Yo', you good?"

"Yes, I am. Did you know that the Feds have you under investigation?"

"Nah, I ain't know and I'm not worried about all that. Right about now my only concern is you. With that said, that bitch ass baby daddy of yours is beginning to be a nuisance."

"I just can't believe he would try to take my kids away from me like that." I shook my head in disbelief.

"Yo, Bianca, fuck all that. Don't put nothing past a fuck nigga. Just tell me what you want me to do and trust me, that shit will be done."

"Jarvis, I can't lose my kids. My kids are my life. I swear, they are."

He waited a few minutes, then he responded. "Look, I live a dangerous lifestyle and I do dangerous things. Some things I can't discuss with you. But, I'm tired of seeing you hurt behind that bitch ass nigga. I done sat back and watched you handle it, but obviously that nigga takes you for a joke. As your nigga, it's my responsibility to protect you."

The rest of the ride was spent in silence, but I wasn't a fool. I knew exactly what Jarvis was referring to. A week ago, murder would've never crossed my mind. But after everything that Mel was putting me through, I would not give a fuck if he disappeared off the face of the earth. It was sad that the man that I once loved was, my number one enemy.

Soon as he pulled up on my block, I noticed that something was off and the neighbors were all outside. When he got closer he got to the house, I realized that there were police cars in front. "Oh God, my aunt," was all I managed to say.

"Yo', what the fuck's' going on?"

"Stop, right here."

"Yo', I'm a bounce up outta here. Hit my phone soon as you know what's going on."

"Ok, Jarvis please be safe."

I got out of his car and he slowly sped off. I rushed up to my driveway where police officers were standing. "This my house. What the hell is going on?" I asked no one in particular.

"What's your name ma'am?"

"Bianca Brown."

"We gave your aunt a copy of the search warrant."

"Search warrant? What the fuck is wrong with y'all people. What the fuck are y'all searching for?"

"Here is a copy of the warrant."

I looked at that asshole, snatched the paper out of his hand and started reading. An informant stated that he bought kilos of cocaine from Jarvis Coleman and I was present. I didn't even bother to finish reading the bullshit that was written on that paper.

"Hey sweetie, there you are. They just busted up in here, scaring the daylight out of me. I don't what the hell is going on here, but somebody's out to get you."

"Melvin Brown auntie. He is behind all of this."

"That son of a bitch needs to be put out of his misery. I can't believe these people are wasting their time on foolishness."

I just stood there as they walked out of the house with bags. What was in them, I didn't know. What I did know was, there had never been any kind of drugs up in my house. Even when Mel was hustling, I was adamant about not having drugs where I laid my head.

After they were finished, they left. I was scared to go inside and face what they'd done. My fucking door was halfway off the hinges and that damn dog tore up most of my shit. I sat on the stairs and literally broke down.

"God ain't goin' give you more than you can bear my child." My aunt rubbed my shoulder as she walked past me.

I had no idea how true that statement was, because I was mentally tired. Losing my kids meant I'd hit rock bottom. Nothing, or no one else mattered to me right about now.

DEVOTED TO A STREET KING
CHAPTER TWENTY-FOUR

Lexi

I called Mel to make sure he was on the block. This dude I was creeping with was on the way over and I swear I could not have them meeting up. See Trigger, and I started creeping around right after my sister had a cook out at her house. We'd managed to keep our relationship on the low, low because he had a bitch and I was messing with Mel. I hadn't even disclosed that to my sister and we shared just about anything.

I took a long shower, shaved my pussy clean and made sure I douched. Homeboy was a freak and his head game was on one thousand. It was something about that nigga and his tongue that made me wet. Just thinking about him had my clit tingling. I got out of the shower, rubbed my body down with lotion and put on a little house dress. I wanted to make sure he didn't have to worry about taking any panties off.

I checked my phone to make sure Mel hadn't called, or sent me any messages. There were none, so that kind of put my mind to rest. I heard the door bell ringing, and jumped up off the couch.

"Whaddup sexy?" He grinned as he walked inside.

"Hey you," I flashed him a little sly grin.

I swear, it was something about that nigga's swag that just made me want to scream. I swear, I'd tried numerous times to put that nigga out of my mind and God knows, I was doing good, until I had to call him in for that favor that I needed. He was the right person, because I knew he was a thug and he would not run his mouth.

"Yo', where yo' man at? I heard you moved that lame ass nigga in."

"Boy, watch your mouth. Ain't nothing lame about my nigga and to answer your question, that nigga is out handling his business, just like I'm about to handle mine." I winked at him and started to pull him up the stairs. I knew I was on borrowed time before the baby woke up.

I wasted no time undressing that nigga, I dropped to my knees and started massaging his soft dick. I started licking the tip of it. "Damn yo', I sure miss this," he said. That only motivated me to use my head skills on him. After I sucked him off and he busted in my mouth, I licked his cum up. He threw me on the bed and placed my legs on his shoulder. He dug his head deep into my love cave and started massaging my clit with his tongue. I placed my hands on the headboard and tried to brace myself for the pleasure I was experiencing. That nigga had me in total bliss. My body shivered as my legs collapsed and I exploded all over his tongue.

"Come on nigga. Give me the dick please," I pleaded to him.

"Hold on, lemme get this rubber. I 'ont want no babies popping out."

"Boy shut up," I chuckled, not giving what he said any thought.

His rock-hard dick entered my wetness. I held on to him and screamed out in ecstasy. I closed my eyes as that nigga rocked my world.

After he busted and I came all over his dick multiple times, we both were tired. I went to use the bathroom and when I came back, I realized that he was not in the room. I didn't have to look far, because he walked in holding my daughter in his arms.

"What are you doing?" I was a little annoyed, because he had no business going in her room.

"Chill out. I heard lil' mama, crying and you were busy handling your business."

"Let me get her." I tried to get her out of his arms.

"Hold on yo! You sure this that nigga's baby?" He moved away, without giving her to me.

"What the fuck you mean nigga? I know who I be fucking." I shot him a confused look.

"I'm just saying shawty. Lil' mama kinda resembles my other daughter and I ain't the smartest nigga, but I know I slept with you right around the same time you conceived."

"Boy, shut the fuck up. This is not your damn baby. You tripping."

"A'ight, prove me wrong and do a DNA test."

"Oh, my God. I can't believe you right now. Matter of fact, give me my child and get out."

I was livid by then. How dare that nigga come up in there talking about some fucking DNA. The thought of Mel finding out that me and that nigga was fucking on the side made my stomach sick.

I snatched my daughter out of his arms, and he left, slamming the door. That nigga had the nerve to have a smile on his face. Did he know what the fuck he'd just started? After I locked the door, I leaned against it with my daughter in my arms. "Oh God, no. There's no possibility!" I screamed out!

CHAPTER TWENTY-FIVE

Bianca

It had been a week and a half since my children had been removed from my care. To make it worse, I had the chance to see them yesterday, but it was supervised. My daughter was crying, because she had no understanding about what was going on. I tried to explain to her that it would be over soon.

My son on the other end was not that receptive. Matter of fact, that little grown ass nigga didn't say one damn word to me. I could see clearly. Mel had his ass brainwashed. It didn't help my pain any, because I was missing them both.

I was under so much pressure that I hadn't eaten in days and all I kept doing was drinking alcohol to numb the pain that I was feeling.

The more I thought about what was going on, the angrier I got. All I thought about was Mel and Lexi, because honestly, I knew her ass was behind all that was taking place. I laid across my bed and all sorts of crazy thoughts popped up in my head. I tried to ignore them, but the more I sipped that wine, the crazier my thoughts became. Tears flowed down my face as I tried to find a little bit of sanity.

I jumped up from the bed, grabbed my gun from my drawer and stormed out of the house. I was about to go see Mel, because I needed answers.

I know that it was early, and there was a chance he was still at that bitch's house. Knowing him, he was going to live with her until she got tired of his ass. I pulled up outside of that bitch's house and saw that I was correct. Mel's vehicle was parked in the driveway behind hers.

I felt my anxiety level rising, but I tried hard to calm myself down. I grabbed my purse and ran up the driveway. I went to the back of the house and tried the windows and they were locked. I ran back to the front and started banging hard on the door like I was the police. I wanted to grab their attention. I stood to the side, waiting for her to open the door.

"Who the fuck's banging on the door like that?" My soon to be ex-husband asked as he opened the door in only his boxers.

"Hey husband! It's only your wife! Now back the fuck up."

"What the fuck are you doing bitch?"

Bap! Bap! Bap! I used all my might to bust that nigga in the face. Blood instantly started pouring from his lip.

He stumbled. "Bitch, I'm gonna kill you!" He tried to run for the stairs.

I fired a shot by his foot. He stopped dead in his tracks. "Babe what the fuck's going on down there? I thought I heard gunshots!"

"Join the party bitch." I pointed the gun at that stupid ass bitch!

Made in the USA
Middletown, DE
10 May 2017